PROFIT AND LOSS

BRUCE DAVIS

Brick Cave Media
brickcavebooks.com

Profit and Loss

PAPERBACK ISBN: 9781938190872
EBOOK ISBN: 9781938190896

Printed in the United States of America.

The characters and events in this book are fictitious. Any
similarity to real persons, living or dead, is coincidental and not
intended by the authors.

Cover Illustration Artist: Thitipon Decruen
www.xric7.com

Brick Cave Media
brickcavebooks.com
2024

Dedication:

For Deuce, you know who you are.

PROFIT AND LOSS

BRUCE DAVIS

Brick Cave Media
brickcavebooks.com

A
RESPECTABLE
PROFIT

Chapter 1

"You have to go down, Zack," Sylvia chided. "It's part of the package."

I heaved myself out of the command chair and picked up the short jacket that was slung over the headrest. "You sound like Cleo, Sylvia," I grumbled. "Never giving a man a minute's peace. Not even in his own cockpit."

"But Cleo told me to make sure you saw our guests off in person."

"You always do what she tells you?" I asked. "I thought I was the captain of this ship."

"You know how she gets when she's cross," Sylvia said. "The passengers are expecting you."

As the *Profit's* Artificial Intelligence, I'd have thought Sylvia immune to Cleo's displeasure. Don't get me wrong. I knew Cleo was the reason we were doing so well lately. I'd lived on the edge of bankruptcy for years until she'd convinced me to take a windfall score and upgrade the *Profit's* passenger cabins and salon. Now, she marketed us to the rich and famous as a high-class charter boat.

It was working, too. The *Profit* was living up to her name for the first time since I'd stolen her from the Martian Navy in the chaos at the end of the Reunification War. I was earning a good living for my crewmates, and myself, and it was all honest money. It was what Cleo had always wanted – a home built on a stable business. I once thought it was what I wanted, too. So why did it chafe on me so?

I shrugged into the 'uniform' jacket. The uniforms were Cleo's idea as well. Made us look more professional, she said. She'd had a hell of a time getting Deuce into one. He refused to wear it except in port and spent most of his time in the engine room or his workshop when passengers were aboard.

"I'm going," I said, putting on my cheerfully confident professional face. I swung through the cockpit hatch and crossed the catwalk above the forward hold. Cleo's voice carried up from the starboard sally port, just below me.

"I'm sure Captain Mbele will be down any second," she said. "And here he is." She shot me a look as I reached the ladder.

I hooked my feet around the ladder railing and slid down, always a sure crowd pleaser. I brushed back a dreadlock that had drifted across my face. The dreadlocks were Cleo's idea, too. She said it made me look sinister, enhancing my reputation as a reformed pirate. I took it in stride. Our bookings were up and the rich charterers paid in cash. If some of them were attracted by the illusion of danger, so what?

"Sorry I'm late." I flashed my best rakish smile. Cleo's eyes said she wasn't buying it. "We had a glitch in the drive gimbals during approach and I had to order a level one overhaul from Port maintenance."

I heard Deuce cough behind me and knew he was covering a guffaw at my technobabble nonsense. I glanced back and saw him standing in the hatch that led aft to the engines and his workshop. His broad shoulders nearly filled the hatchway, his smooth scalp and blond beard set off by the black and gold uniform jacket. He nodded to me but made no move to come forward and join us. Not that the passengers would expect it.

"I was telling the Guthrie's how much we enjoyed having them with us for this trip." Cleo looped her arm through mine, poking me hard in the ribs at the same time.

I managed not to grunt at her poke and smiled again. "Yes, indeed. A real pleasure."

I reached out with my free right hand and grasped Mr. Guthrie's. His grip was firm and sure, just what I would have expected from a self-made ice merchant. Sam Guthrie had made a fortune in a cutthroat business and wasn't impressed with our playacting. He and I had shared a few drinks late in the sleep cycle while we told war stories about our service on opposite sides in the Reunification War. I liked the man.

"Oh, Captain Mbele," gushed his wife. "Will Mr. Conejo be coming down to say good-bye? I simply must get that spiced fishcake recipe before we leave."

Mrs. Guthrie was much younger than her husband and excelled at looking perfect (and at spending his money). She and her daughter, Ingrid, were the rest of our little charter group. Cleo had spent much of the trip keeping the two of them away from Deuce and me. Me because my tolerance for Mrs. Guthrie's brand of self-important silliness was marginal, and Deuce because Ingrid was seventeen, looked twenty-five, and liked playing seduction games with big, tough men. There wasn't much fear that Deuce would take her up on it, but why take the chance?

"I'm sure Rabbit, that is Mr. Conejo, would be here if he could," I said. "He's busy in the galley and it's hard for him to negotiate the ladder from the upper deck in his wheelchair." In fact, Rabbit's fancy power chair could descend the ladder as fast as anyone. I knew he was hiding in his cabin. "I'll have Sylvia download the recipe to your link. Rabbit wanted you to have it. Sylvia?"

"Done, Zack," she replied.

"Tell him thank you for me," Mrs. Guthrie said. "His meals were the best part of this trip."

One of the surprises of our new 'respectability' was the discovery of Rabbit's talent in the galley. He'd always seemed indifferent to food, eating only for sustenance. But he approached cooking in the same analytical way he approached programming or data slicing. The result was near perfection as long as he had a recipe to follow.

The cargo 'bots arrived along with a deferential customs inspector to offload our charges' luggage. The inspector's obsequious fawning was a sharp contrast to the handling we'd received on our last visit to the Highpoint arcology, one of several massive LaGrange point space stations parked at L5. That time we'd been swindled out of our shipping fee, part of the cargo, and nearly the *Profit* as well. Respectability had its perks.

Cleo and I edged the ladies toward the sally port. Guthrie strode ahead, ready to be off. Just as we reached the lock, Mrs. Guthrie pulled out a holorecorder and turned to me.

"Please, Captain," she said. "Just one hologram of you and Ingrid. As a keepsake."

Cleo glared at me as she released my arm.

"Of course," I said, returning Cleo's look.

Ingrid stepped up next to me and snuggled under my arm. She made a point of pressing her breast against my side and snaked her arm around my waist. Her finger played up and down my back under the short jacket as her mother fussed with the recorder and finally got the image she wanted. She smiled her thanks and began putting the recorder away. Ingrid snuggled closer. I gently disengaged her arm and stepped away, drawing a small pout from her. Cleo looked daggers at her, but if Ingrid noticed, she hid it well.

"Well, that's all then," said Cleo cheerfully, leading them to the lock. Mr. Guthrie was already at the foot of the sally port stairs. He threw me a short nod as his wife took his arm and they strode off across the docking bay with Ingrid in tow.

"Did you enjoy your little cuddle, lover boy?" Cleo asked as she waved to the Guthrie's.

"Should I have tossed her off the ship?"

"No, but you didn't have to enjoy yourself so much." She elbowed my ribs again. "You'll make it up to me tonight."

I pulled her closer. "Yes, ma'am."

She kissed my cheek, then pulled away. "Not now. I

need to log their payment and put our name on the open charter list. With luck, we can pick up a client and not have to deadhead back to Tycho."

I had been looking forward to having Cleo to myself on the passage back to our homeport of Tycho City on the Moon but didn't say so. Cleo was more than my ex-wife and current business partner, but we still weren't quite back to husband and wife yet. She had always craved the security of a successful business and, for the time being, I was willing to go along. Especially since the alternative was losing her.

I watched her climb the ladder to the upper deck and sighed. I owned the ship outright, we paid our bills on time, and we were welcome most everywhere we went. (Well, not on Ceres or Kwai Hong One, but you can't please everyone.) Yes, being respectable had a lot going for it. Too bad it was so damn boring.

Deuce reappeared in the aft hatch, minus the uniform jacket. "We pickin' up more passengers, LT?" He pronounced each letter, El Tee, a holdover from our days in the Martian Special Forces.

"Don't know, Deuce. Cleo's fishing for jobs, but if no one steps up, we'll be empty on the run back to Tycho."

"That'd suit me fine," he said, rubbing his smooth scalp. "Okay if I take a little shore leave while we're in port? I'm gettin' a bit cramped back here."

"Sure. Just stay in touch through your link and stay sober."

"No fear, LT." Deuce grinned.

"Never, Deuce."

I left him and climbed the ladder to the upper deck. Cleo was in our quarters working at the holomatrix. I went forward to the cockpit and shed the jacket before dropping into the command chair. From there I could look out on the huge docking bay that housed the *Profit*. At sixty meters length and four thousand metric tons capacity, she was small for a freighter and occupied less than a third of the space in the bay. I watched Deuce leave through the main lock, off on his own business.

A thought occurred to me, and I checked the bay

identifier posted above the main exit lock: Bay 42, spinward. I smiled. The same berth we'd had more than three years earlier.

"Sylvia, see if you can get Akira Kensai on the comm. Senior Patrol Officer Akira Kensai, unless he's been promoted since our last visit."

"Right away, Boss."

A few seconds later, the contact lens in my left eye flickered and an image of a tallish man with close cropped black hair and brown, almond-shaped eyes appeared. He peered at me through the cockpit video pickup.

"Hello," I said. "I'm trying to reach Akira Kensai. Is he available?"

"I'm Tanaka Kensai," he said. "Akira was my brother."

"Was?"

"My brother was killed in the line of duty almost two years ago. May I ask who you are?"

I sat back in the command chair. Akira Kensai dead? The last honest cop in Highpoint? We'd crossed paths three years before, when I'd given him the evidence to bust the crooked customs operation that had robbed us. The bust hadn't made him popular with the authorities. Not that he'd cared. Corruption and graft may have been art forms on Highpoint, but Kensai kept himself above it. I'd trusted him, ultimately with my life.

I shook my head to clear it. "I'm Zachariah Mbele," I said. "I knew your brother when he was a Senior Patrol Officer. I'm sorry to hear that he's dead; sorry for your loss. How did it happen?"

"He was killed while breaking up a jolt smuggling deal. At least, that's the official version. But Akira wouldn't have gone in without backup, and no drugs were ever found." He paused. "Mbele? The ship captain?"

"Yes," I said warily. "How do you know that?"

"Akira told be about you," he said. "You were the one who gave him the glowgem formula; and took out a squad of renegade Martian commandos who were after it. He said you were either the luckiest or the most dangerous man he'd ever met." He took a deep breath before speaking more slowly. "I'd like to meet with you while you're here in

Highpoint. Akira told me you didn't mind breaking some rules."

I shook my head. "Maybe in the old days. I'm out of the smuggling game now. I run a respectable charter operation."

"Please, Mr. Mbele. I'm not asking you to do anything illegal. I found something in Akira's files about Fingol Malloy. You gave Aki the original files on culturing glowgems. Maybe you can understand what it's about."

Three years earlier I'd given Kensai the notebooks of Fingol Malloy, a half-crazy xenobiologist turned prospector who'd figured out how to grow cultured glowgems. Natural glowgems were silicon crystals that looked like nondescript quartz in the cold of space but glowed with their own light when warmed to twenty degrees Celsius. They had once been among the most valuable and sought after items in the solar system; until the technique of culturing them was made public, that is. I'd given Kensai the secret knowing he'd release it to the media and remove any motive for the Red Dragons to kill me for it.

"What about Fingol Malloy?" I asked.

"I'll tell you about it in person. Three o'clock this afternoon, lobby of the Imperial Hotel, Garden Level." He broke the connection.

I sat back in the chair. Kensai's death was a surprise. He hadn't been a friend, exactly, but we'd arrived at a level of mutual respect that some friends never reach. It would be like him to keep digging into Malloy's story, even after the secret of cultured glowgems went public.

"Zack, are you okay?" Sylvia asked after several minutes.

"I'm fine, Sylvia." I stood and headed aft. "Is Cleo still in our cabin?"

"Yes, Boss. You want me to call her?"

"No, I'm headed that way. Call up a map of the arcology and find the Imperial Hotel. Download directions to my link."

"Don't you believe Officer Kensai was killed by jolt smugglers?" Sylvia asked.

"Eavesdropping again?"

"It's my duty to monitor the com channels," she said in her officious voice, the one she used when she'd overstepped her bounds and got defensive when called on it. "Besides, you asked me to get *Akira* Kensai. I had to make sure I had the right person on the com."

I wondered for the thousandth time why I'd let Rabbit program an AI with a female personality. The emotion and response algorithms he'd installed in her were so good that Sylvia could pass for human. She even claimed to be in love with me, a concept I found hard to fathom.

"Sure you did," I said. "But, for what it's worth, no. I'm not sure I do believe it. Kensai was a good cop, and even the best get sloppy occasionally. Still, I don't see him deliberately going into a dangerous situation without backup. He made some powerful enemies with the customs bust, but from what I heard, most of them are still doing hard time in Antarctica. Maybe Tanaka can tell me more."

"The location is in your map locator. Be careful, Zack. If Kensai's superiors had him killed over that customs raid three years ago, they won't hesitate to kill you for giving him the evidence."

"You're acting like a mother hen, Sylvia. It was three years ago. I can't see anyone taking action after that much time. Bad for business. Besides, I'm always careful. It's my nature."

"Sure you are," she said in a tone suspiciously like Cleo's, a bit of programming I reminded myself to have Rabbit remove. "Seriously, Zack, if the people who run this place had Kensai killed, what makes you think we're safe here?"

I didn't answer her because I agreed with her. I just hoped she was wrong. I swung through the hatch and crossed the catwalk. Rabbit was in the salon absorbed in his virtual keyboard and a holomatrix full of code. I found Cleo still in front of the matrix in our shared quarters.

She looked up as I came in. "We cleared twenty-seven hundred yuan on that last run. Not bad for three days' work. I posted us on the open charter board, but it doesn't look good. There are six ships ahead of us on the list."

"How long do you mean to wait?"

She shrugged. "A couple of days. We have some ready cash and can stock up on some luxury provisions while we're here."

"Good. I let Deuce go ashore to blow off some steam. And I'm going to meet Tanaka Kensai at the Imperial at three today." I didn't mention Fingol Malloy.

"Kensai? The cop?" she asked.

I shook my head. "His brother. Akira Kensai is dead. Killed in a drug raid gone bad, apparently. I'm hoping Tanaka can tell me more."

"I didn't realize the two of you were close," she said. "I spent most of my time back then trying to avoid him."

I smiled. "That's because you were a fugitive, darling. But, no, we weren't close. I respected him and trusted him. I'm sorry he's dead."

She nodded. "I hope you find out what happened. He sounds like he was a good man."

"I'll be home before dinner, I expect."

She nodded absently, already absorbed in the business accounts. I opened the clothing locker and put on a clean black shirt and short, loose-sleeved jacket. I kissed Cleo on the top of her head and left the cabin.

I stopped at the weapons locker on the main deck. With all the passengers aboard, we'd had to install DNA locks so that only crew could open it. I thumbed the lock and drew out a slim Smith and Wesson needler with a pneumatic boost and an extra magazine of sleepers. The needler went into a shoulder holster sewn into the jacket lining, the magazine into an inner jacket pocket. I strapped a wrist sheath to my right arm and added a chrome steel throwing knife. Maybe it was overkill, but I never left the ship unarmed and I didn't know Tanaka. He might be like his brother, but he might not.

I adjusted the jacket sleeves and made sure the knife dropped smoothly into my palm with the flick of my wrist. I nudged my nanofibers to low level activity and felt the familiar itchy tingle as they extended through my nerve sheaths.

The nanos were a gift of the Martian revolution, as

well. Deuce and I had been part of Hans Metternich's infamous Third Directorate, in the counterinsurgency Special Forces, prior to the revolution against the Federal Republic that started the Reunification War. Metternich had risen to power on a wave of Martian Way zealotry only to drive the Revolution into madness and tyranny with his dream of creating a race of superhuman soldiers through nanotechnology. Thousands had been imprisoned and killed in his human experiments to bond nanofibers to the human nervous system. Only a few, one in one hundred thousand, had the right protein in the myelin nerve sheath to accept a stable bond with the nanos. I was the only survivor of his biotanks that I knew of with a complete stable bond. A few, like Rabbit, had partial bonds that left them alive but with permanent nerve damage. Rabbit was paralyzed from the waist down but could use his nanos to control his powered wheelchair.

I shrugged my shoulders to settle the needler in its hidden holster, undogged the starboard sally port lock and swung the hatch inward. The boarding ladder extended automatically. I climbed down to the deck of the cargo bay and set off for the spaceport exit.

The Imperial wasn't hard to find. It was the biggest hotel on the Garden Level, the huge open central core of the arcology. I caught a tube from the spaceport to the entertainment mall under the hotel and avoided the open space of the central core. I'm a tunnel rat from Mars. Open space gives me the shakes.

I climbed a broad staircase sheathed in faux marble to the lobby level, avoiding the dropshafts and bounce tubes. The stairs gave me a better field of view and I didn't have to stand still in a crowd of people. Besides, the exercise was supposed to be good for me. Success had a way of making one soft.

The staircase topped out in a broad landing. To my left, wide doors led out onto the green belt that bordered the Esplanade, the arcology's upscale shopping and entertainment district. To the right, glowing holographic letters in tasteful royal blue directed me to the Imperial Hotel.

The Imperial's lobby opened up into a massive atrium that soared high above the main floor and was unroofed at the top. So much for avoiding open spaces. If I chose, I could look up and see the curving green of the opposite side of the arcology's three-kilometer wide cylinder. I didn't choose to look and hurried across the lobby toward an alcove that my maplink identified as the bar.

I recognized Tanaka before he saw me. He sat in a low overstuffed chair next to a faux-stone table near the shining, copper-topped bar. The chair was too low and made it impossible for him to stand quickly. That marked him as untrained. He wasn't his brother. I walked up behind him, unnoticed in the crowded barroom.

"Mr. Kensai," I said. He jumped, startled. "I'm Zack Mbele. What did you want to talk to me about?"

He struggled out of the chair and wiped a sweaty palm on his trousers before offering his hand. I shook it. His grip was strong, but he was nervous. I didn't know what Akira had told him, but I doubted he was afraid of me. Something else had him twitchy.

"Sit down," he said.

"Not here." I pointed to the bar. "Over there." I led him to a pair of high barstools. He sat facing the bar, his hands on the smooth copper sheathing of the bar top. I leaned against my chair, my hands free at my sides, so that I could see the door and the rest of the lobby.

Tanaka ordered Martian whiskey, neat, and turned to me. "What are you drinking?

"McAllen single malt, water on the side."

The flesh and blood bartender (this was a luxury hotel, after all; no AI, serving 'bots in sight) was quick and deferential as he set the drinks in front of us.

"On the same tab, Mr. Kensai?"

"Fine, Walter," he said. He obviously came here often enough that the staff knew him.

I splashed a few drops of water into my scotch and took a sip. It was the 18-year-old line, smooth and slightly floral. Tanaka knocked his drink back in a single gulp and waved a finger at Walter for a refill.

I waited until Walter had exchanged his glass and then

Bruce Davis

asked, "What did you want to talk about, Mr. Kensai?" I figured I had better find out what this was about before he was too drunk to tell me.

He sipped the whiskey this time before answering. "Three years ago, you gave my brother some detailed financial information on a crooked customs official. It led him and his team to a major bribery and theft ring involving some very high officials in the Highpoint Department of Commerce. He made Captain as a result of that case, but he also made some dangerous enemies."

I said nothing, waiting for him to continue.

"Aki never told me how you got the financial data. Maybe, he never knew. I do know enough about banking law to know that it wasn't obtained legally. Plus, it was never presented to a Magistrate, or used at trial. It was obviously real, since it let Akira find the money trail to the ringleaders. So, where did it come from?"

"Why do you want to know?" I sipped my drink and surveyed the room again. I wasn't about to confess to illegally slicing into privileged financial records in a public place.

He didn't answer directly but said, "I also know you gave Aki the Fingol Malloy files at around the same time. Aki could have used them to get rich, but that wasn't his way. He made them public shortly after he got them." He finally looked at me. "You knew he would, didn't you? Just like you knew he'd go after the big fish in the customs investigation, no matter what it cost." I didn't say anything to that, either, and he went on, "After the files went public, he kept investigating Malloy. Even as a kid, he'd been a Fingol's Cave buff. He found references to another report about the gems, something important enough to be classified."

I shrugged. "So, what? Malloy was half crazy when he died. Nobody even knew about the files until a data slicer dug them up while raiding dead safe deposit boxes."

"Aki was convinced there was something important in that report. Malloy filed it with the Feds before he did the research on culturing the gems."

I was getting impatient with this ramble "So it's in the

20

Federal database. What does that have to do with me?"

"The report isn't in the database," Tanaka said. "Aki searched for it. He paid a datamining service to look for it. He even used his own security clearance to search. He finally found a reference tag in an old purge report."

"They purged it?" I was interested now. Data purges were a sure sign that somebody wanted the file buried and forgotten.

Tanaka nodded. "Just before Aki died, he sent me a message along with his files on Malloy. He told me to keep them safe. I think he was expecting trouble. He died a few days later."

"You think he knew someone was after him?" I asked.

Tanaka nodded. "We weren't all that close, Mr. Mbele. It wasn't usual for Aki to contact me, much less give me something to keep for him. He knew his life was in danger. I'm sure of it."

"Where are Akira's files now?"

Tanaka patted his breast pocket. "I keep a datastick with the files on my person all the time. Another is in a safe deposit box under a numbered account at a bank here on Highpoint."

"Stupid to keep the files on you," I said. "Anyone could take you down and get them."

"Only if they know I'm carrying them. And if they kill me to get them, then I won't really care anymore, will I?" He shrugged with a wry smile. "I was never as driven or as principled as Aki. He was the older brother, the one expected to carry on the family name and honor. I've always been in his shadow. This is my chance to do something Aki would have done."

"Do what?"

"Follow the trail Aki started on. Find Fingol Malloy's original report and make sense of his legacy. The original report was filed at an old Federal base on Ceres. Shortly afterwards, the base was sold to Kwai Hong Holdings. Aki thought the original report was still there, buried in the old database on the main Ceres server. You, or someone on your crew, obviously can slice into high-level encryptions and retrieve sensitive data. I thought you or your slicer might know how to slice that database."

At the mention of Kwai Hong, I felt a chill and my nanofibers twitched. A few months before, I'd almost died at the hands of Kwai Chang Wu, old Kwai Hong's number-two son. Wu had ended up dead instead of me and, as far as I knew, only the *Profit's* crew knew Deuce had killed him. But rumor had it that Kwai wanted me dead and wasn't particular about who did the job. The *Profit* avoided Ceres and Kwai Hong One, the company's LaGrange satellite, and we gave Kwai Hong ships a wide berth.

I flexed my hands, feeling the nanofibers bonded to my central nervous system augment my speed and strength. My vision shifted to infrared and I scanned the room for threats. Just the mention of Kwai Hong shouldn't have affected me so. I looked about more carefully. Something in the room had subconsciously triggered the nano response; something that my body registered as a threat even though my brain hadn't processed it yet.

Tanaka noticed my expression and looked around. "What is it?"

"I don't know," I said, scanning the room. "Come on, we're getting out of here."

He nodded and slid off the barstool. I caught a flash of motion from the open space of the lobby. The needler leapt into my right hand as I pushed Tanaka down with my left. My augmented vision picked up a glow of heat to our right. I ducked as a pneumatic round whizzed past my ear. I fell back behind the corner of the bar, dragging Tanaka with me and returning fire. A thick-necked man in a light blue shirt dove behind a table as my needles embedded themselves in the tabletop. He held a long barrel Steinbauer pneumatic in his hand.

"What's happening?" Tanaka babbled. "Is someone shooting at us? Where is he?"

I shoved him down as he started to rise to look over the bar. Pneumatic rounds pinged off of the copper bar top. I stuck my head around the edge of the bar and caught a glimpse of the man in the blue shirt sidling to the right along a thickly padded couch, trying to get a shot around the corner where I crouched.

I glanced behind me. There was an exit to the shopping district about five meters to the left and behind the bar. There were a half dozen small tables and groupings of low chairs that offered scant cover between our position and the exit.

I pointed that way. "Go. Stay low, crawl if you have to. When you get to the exit run toward the tube stations. I'll catch up."

He opened his mouth to say something but two more rounds punched through the bar and splintered the barstool next to his head. He hunched low and scurried on hands and knees to the first cluster of chairs.

I popped up over the top of the bar and fired toward where I'd last seen the gunman. He ducked behind the couch and my needles stuck in the faux leather where he had been a fraction of a second earlier. My infrared augmented vision caught a trace of heat signature as he moved to the left, away from the nearest line of sight, but possibly toward a less expected position. I moved with him, needler up and tracking along the couch. When he popped up to take his shot, my finger was already squeezing trigger.

Both needles caught him in the neck, one dead center, the other just below his left ear. He managed to get off a shot before the drug hit his brain and he slumped to the floor. The round thumped solidly into the copper bar top, gouging a deep furrow before embedding itself in the underlying polyplast backing.

I leaped over the bar and rushed to the now inert gunman. I checked the pulse in his neck. Weak and thready but palpable. I pulled the Steinbauer from his grip and tucked it into my waistband before patting him down quickly. As expected, the only things he carried were a couple of extra magazines for the pneumatic and a transit pass for the tube system. No identification or cash. He was a professional on a job, traveling sterile. I turned and headed for the exit.

I found Tanaka crouching behind a table a few steps from the exit. I hauled him to his feet and shoved him ahead of me. We made it out the rear lobby entrance and down the ramp onto the greenbelt before the alarms started to sound in the hotel lobby. I wove in and out of the crowd, sometimes pushing Tanaka ahead, sometimes pulling him along. He followed without a word, his face pale. Definitely nothing like his brother. We reached the tube station, and I ducked behind a support column and checked our tail. Nothing there.

I considered our next move. By now the local cops were all over the lobby bar. It wasn't likely that anyone would know me, but Tanaka was no stranger to the bartender. Walter would also be able to give a decent description of me, and I was certain half a dozen public safety surveillance cameras both in the bar and on our way here had recorded us. Not much point in trying to disappear.

I decided we'd play it open. I was a respectable businessman. Tanaka was...whatever he was here. I'd been attacked and had wisely run away. No one had been killed. I might have a hard time explaining the Steinbauer and the throwing knife, but a needler loaded with sleeper darts was a legal self-defense weapon, even here on Highpoint. We'd go back to the ship and wait for the authorities to contact us.

Neither of us spoke on the way back to the spaceport. Tanaka still seemed stunned by the attack and I didn't have a clue who had fired at me. It wasn't like I didn't have enemies. Kwai Hong was just the most outspoken. The Red Dragons were consumed by infighting but might come together long enough to agree on hitting me. But how would either of them know where I'd be? Hell, they shouldn't even know I was on Highpoint.

No one waited for us at the main terminal. No one stopped us on the way to the ship. Tanaka seemed to loosen up as we entered the docking bay. I didn't feel any better. I pulled the Steinbauer pneumatic from my waistband again as Tanaka walked in front of me. He looked back at me as he reached the foot of the sally port stairs and froze when he saw the pneumatic.

"Up the ladder," I said. He hesitated and I shoved the

pneumatic under his chin. "Do it now! I've shot people I like better than you. Someone just tried to kill me and I want to know why."

"I don't know anything about that," he said, raising his arms.

"No one else knew about our meeting. That shooter couldn't have known I'd be there unless you tipped him off."

"But I told no one." His voice was shaky, but he didn't avoid my eyes. "You called me. I didn't even know you'd be on Highpoint."

He was right. Even if he'd tipped someone off, they'd need to have a gunman in place waiting for the call, which didn't make sense. Unless I wasn't the target. I lowered the pneumatic.

"Get into the ship," I said. "Somebody wants you dead, and I want to know who it is."

Chapter 2

Tanaka may have not have been a cop, but he wasn't stupid. He came to the same conclusion I had and scrambled up the ladder. I followed and sealed the sally port behind me.

"Up to the salon." I pointed to the upper deck. "Sylvia, security lockdown"

"Initiating, Boss."

Tanaka climbed the ladder to the upper deck. I followed and directed him to the salon. He looked around with evident curiosity. It had always been the focal point of the living quarters, a combination living space and dining compartment. Since our big payoff from the Dragons, Cleo and Sylvia had redecorated it in soft, earthy tones with pastel fabric covering the bulkheads, overstuffed chairs, and a big active contour sofa in the center. On one bulkhead, a holomatrix provided music, entertainment, and link access to Sylvia's database. On the opposite bulkhead hung a complex glass sculpture, a Diego Salazar original, that may or may not have been stolen. It had been a wedding gift from Rabbit when Cleo and I had gotten married the first time. Rabbit wasn't too specific about its provenance and warned me not to try to have it appraised.

I waved toward a chair under the Salazar wall sculpture. "Sit," I said to Tanaka. Then I spoke to Sylvia's audio pickup. "Sylvia, find Rabbit and have him join us in the salon. And where is Deuce?"

"Deuce's link shows him to be on the Esplanade, Garden level. At a club called the Planetia. Do you want me to call him?"

I thought for a moment. Deuce was capable of taking care of himself. This was about Tanaka. There was no reason to suspect a general attack on the ship or crew. "No, not yet. But keep track of his whereabouts."

"Yes, Boss."

Rabbit rolled in a few minutes later and looked curiously at Tanaka. "What's up, Zack? Who's this?"

I made the introductions. "Tanaka Kensai, this is Eddie Conejo, Rabbit to his friends. Rabbit, Tanaka is Akira Kensai's brother. Somebody just took a shot at him at the Imperial Hotel. Almost shot me instead."

"Geez, Zack," Rabbit said. "Why'd you bring him here? I mean, no offense and all, but I thought we gave that kind of stuff up after the Wu job. I kind of miss it, but since Cleo took over the business, things have been a lot calmer around here."

"Never mind why," I said. "Do you still have your backdoor access to the Highpoint security grid?"

He grinned. "Unless they found someone with more smarts than me to upgrade their systems, I can open it in thirty seconds."

"Do it. Check on the shooting at the Imperial. See if you can find out who that hitter was and whether the cops are looking for me or Tanaka."

Rabbit opened a virtual keyboard in the air in front of his powerchair and his fingers danced through the air for a few seconds. The holomatrix along the starboard bulkhead lit up with lines of text and video feeds from a dozen security cameras.

After a few seconds, he enlarged a couple of the feeds to a split screen. One showed the bar at the Imperial.

Technicians in pale blue coveralls with HPS stenciled across the back swarmed over the bar and tables, measuring, scanning, and imaging the scene of our brief gun battle. The second feed focused on the approach to the cargo terminal. A squad of six blue uniformed Highpoint Security officers double-timed along the concourse led by a large man in a well fitted black business suit.

"I think the Highpoint cops are looking for you, Zack." Rabbit waved a hand and my picture and a brief dossier appeared in a separate window. "They identified you from the security cam in the Imperial. The team is on its way here."

I studied the guy in the suit. He was obviously in charge, a Senior Patrol Officer or higher, maybe an Inspector. I didn't think anything I'd done would warrant that much juice. I'd been packing sleepers, after all. The guy who had tried to kill us was the one shooting lethal ammunition.

"Tanaka, have you ever seen this guy before?" I asked.

He looked closely at the matrix and nodded. "That's Kamil Ghosh. He was Aki's partner before Aki was killed. He moved up and took over Aki's job afterwards."

"Did he have a problem with Akira?"

Tanaka shrugged. "I don't know. Like I said, Aki and I weren't close. Ghosh came to the funeral, though. He seemed genuinely upset. He told me Akira had sent him over to the spinward side to run down an informant the night of the drug bust. It turned out to be a false trail. That's why he wasn't there when Aki was killed."

"Is he honest?"

Tanaka smiled sadly. "This is Highpoint, Mbele. Define honest."

"Do you think he might have been working for the people who had Akira killed?" I asked, watching the monitor. The security team was nearing our bay. I would need to make a decision soon.

Tanaka shook his head. "No. Like I said, he seemed genuinely upset that my brother was dead, and the inquest showed that he'd received a valid order from Aki over his link."

I knew it might be too much to hope that Ghosh was as honest as Akira Kensai had been, but it looked like he'd been Kensai's partner and possibly his protégé. If his corruption was merely venal, he might be open to persuasion that I was defending myself in the shooting at the Imperial. For once, I could use my past reputation to my advantage and not feel like a whore for doing it.

Sylvia called a few seconds later. "We're being hailed, Zack. A Senior Patrol Officer Ghosh is demanding I open up and let him and his team board us."

"Put him through to the salon screen, Sylvia. And ask Cleo to please join us here."

A half second later the matrix lit up with a view of the docking bay taken from one of *Profit's* exterior cameras high above the deck. Sylvia zoomed in on Ghosh who looked annoyed but not really angry; not yet, anyway.

"SP Ghosh," I said. "To what do we owe this pleasure?"

"Zachariah Mbele," Ghosh's tone was serious and formal, but my augmented hearing picked up the underlying nervous quaver in his pronunciation of my name. "I have an order to detain you and Mr. Tanaka Kensai for questioning in a criminal matter. We know Kensai is aboard. Open your lock and allow my team access to your ship."

"Do you have a search warrant? Or is this a criminal arrest?" I asked, my voice pleasant and tone carefully neutral.

Ghosh looked nonplussed. "No."

"Then I'm afraid I can't allow you or your team to board. I am willing to speak to you about what happened in the Imperial Hotel, but only through this link or outside the ship. If you wish to detain me at that point, you may do so, but without a warrant, I categorically forbid any boarding of this ship."

"Where is Tanaka Kensai?" Ghosh asked.

I noticed he didn't say anything about my invocation of basic Federation rights. I may not be happy with the current group of thugs running the government, but I was well versed in the Federation Charter and its basic guarantees. Ghosh seemed more interested in Tanaka than in me. *Curious,* I thought. I wondered if Akira had told him about his encounters with me. This conversation was almost a replay of the last meeting I'd had with Akira, right here in this bay.

"Mr. Kensai is a guest aboard this ship," I said. "And any protections invoked apply to him as well. He may choose of his own free will to speak with you, but without a warrant, I won't compel him to do so."

"I can get a warrant in ten minutes, if that's the way you want it." He tried to look hard and confident but failed on both counts.

"Why are you talking to a policeman about warrants, Zack?" Cleo asked quietly from the salon hatch. I hadn't heard her approach, but it was just as well she was there. Ghosh and I had reached the point where I'd have to give a little or call his bluff. For all I knew, at this point, he might be able to get that warrant.

"I'm sure you can, sir," I said to Ghosh as I held up one finger toward Cleo. "But a Magistrate is going to want to know why you were unwilling to take our statements outside of my ship." I held Cleo's questioning eye for a moment, then said, "Look, why don't I save us both a lot of trouble. I'll come out into the bay and discuss the attack on my person at the Imperial Hotel. I will also ask, ASK, Mr. Kensai if he is willing to accompany me. Will that be acceptable?"

Ghosh looked as if he'd just bitten into something sour, but he shrugged and said, "Have it your way. Outside, both of you."

I glanced at Tanaka. He nodded. "Agreed," I told Ghosh and broke the connection.

Cleo stood in the hatchway with her hands on her hips. "Who is this?" She inclined her head toward Tanaka. "And why do you need to talk to the police?"

"Cleopatra Lee, this is Tanaka Kensai, Akira Kensai's brother," I said, making the introductions. "Tanaka had a bit of trouble in the bar at the Imperial Hotel. Shots may have been fired. Senior Patrol Officer Ghosh is here to take our statements."

Cleo gave Tanaka an appraising glance and then

stepped closer to whisper in my ear. "What's going on, Zack? Did the Dragons make a run at you?"

I shook my head and whispered back, "No. Tanaka was the target. I put a couple of sleepers into the shooter and we hustled back here. Ghosh, the cop outside, was Akira's partner. Tanaka seems to think he's on the square. If we're going to play the part of law-abiding citizens, I need to give the authorities a statement. It shouldn't take long."

She eyed Tanaka again. He returned her gaze, but he looked pale and frightened.

"All right," she said. "But we're a charter boat now, not a crew of pirates. Don't get carried away with one of your freedom and constitutional rights rants."

I smiled. "No fear, darling. I'll be the soul of discretion."

She grimaced. "Spare me. Just watch your mouth. We've worked hard to build a reputation. Getting jammed up with the cops won't look good."

"Bull," I said. "Part of the allure you've worked so hard to build is our reputation as a bunch of reformed pirates. As long as I don't get thrown in the brig, a conversation with Ghosh only enhances that." I cocked my head. "You aren't worried about our rep, are you?"

She didn't speak, just put her hands on either side of my face and kissed me. Then she turned and left the compartment.

I shook my head. There was a time when I'd had to hold a gun to her head before she'd admit she loved me. This concern was out of character and confusing. I didn't need to be confused if I was facing a police grilling. I knew I'd done nothing illegal, but this was Highpoint, and I didn't know for sure that the very authorities I was going to talk to hadn't ordered Tanaka's death in the first place.

"Rabbit, can you track and record this meeting through my link?"

"No problem, Zack. Even if they disable it with a scrambler, I have access to their security net. I can follow you into their most secure interrogation room if I want to."

"I don't think it will come to that. Just make sure

we have a record of everything that happens to me or to Tanaka."

I waved a hand at Tanaka, and he followed me down to the main deck. I popped the airlock seal on the starboard sally port and spun the dogs to release the hatch.

I swung it inward and called out, "Ghosh? Two coming out."

I descended the ladder first, followed by Tanaka. Ghosh stepped forward and waved his team back when they started to follow. He stopped in front of me and extended his hand.

"Mr. Mbele, I'm Kamil Ghosh. Thank you for agreeing to speak with me." He was now every inch the respectful public servant, but his eyes were hard. He assessed me with a professional gaze, stopping for an instant at my left armpit and my right sleeve. He knew where I carried my weapons.

"I'll help any way I can," I said, shaking his hand. "But I'm afraid I can't tell you very much." I turned slightly and indicated Tanaka. "You know Mr. Kensai, I believe?"

Ghosh nodded to him. "How are you, Tanaka. It's been a while."

"Two years, since the funeral," said Tanaka. "Any progress on Aki's case?"

Ghosh grimaced. "It's still an open file, but I've been instructed to 'work on higher priority investigations' until new leads are developed."

"And so you've stopped looking."

"I've done everything I can for now," Ghosh said with a resigned sigh. "I know you think I've given up, but I've pulled every string I can and called in every marker I can think of. No one is willing to push this thing any further. I'm sorry, Tanaka. I really am."

Tanaka made a noncommittal grunt and nodded. Ghosh put on his official face and said in a more formal tone, "Why would a paid assassin try to shoot you in a public place?"

"I don't know," said Tanaka with a trace of indignation that sounded forced to me. "Why don't you ask Mr. Mbele? He's the one with the reputation. Maybe some old enemies are trying to even the score."

Ghosh shook his head. "The security images show clearly that he was aiming at you, not Mbele. The trajectory analysis of his first shot shows you were the intended target. It was only after Mbele engaged him that he shifted his focus. Who wants you dead?"

"I don't know," repeated Tanaka.

"The gunman's name was Ian Sayer. Does that name mean anything to you?"

Tanaka shook his head. "Never heard of him."

Ghosh looked at me. "What about you, Mbele."

I noticed that once we were outside and clearly under the control of his squad, he had dropped the polite pretense of *Mr. Mbele.* I shook my head as well. "Did he have any identifying marks?" I asked.

Ghosh smiled. "No Dragon tattoo on his left palm, if that's what you're asking. He was from Gagarin Center, suspected in a number of killings all over the Moon and two on Mars. No convictions, but he was regarded as a known hired killer."

"Freelancer then, hired by someone else." I paused. "Wait, 'was'? What do you mean 'was'?"

"He's dead," said Ghosh. "He was unresponsive when the paramedics arrived. They gave him reversal agents for all of the common sleeper needles, but he didn't respond."

"So wait an hour for the drugs to wear off," I said. "Two needles shouldn't have killed him."

"Shouldn't have, but did," Ghosh answered. "And before you ask, there are no charges against you. It was clearly self-defense, and you were using non-lethal ammunition. The coroner will determine the cause of death, and you'll be informed if any further charges are developed from that information." He turned slightly and indicated the small personnel lock next to the main bay doors. "Now, just go with the Sergeant and we'll record your statements at the substation."

"Why not here?" I asked. Sayer's death made my confidence in the self-defense scenario shaky. I didn't want to suddenly find myself in a police lockup waiting for the coroner to file his report.

"Procedure," said Ghosh. "Official records or witness interviews are to be done in secure facilities whenever possible to reduce the risk of tampering or unauthorized access."

His explanation was bullshit, but outside the ship, with a squad of armed men backing him up, there wasn't much to be gained by protesting. There was no way that my two needles should have been fatal to a 90-year-old grandmother, much less a professional assassin. I needed to find out how he'd died and who had arranged it. Someone with some heavy juice wanted Tanaka dead and didn't want any troublesome witnesses. Besides, I was a law abiding Federation citizen, cooperating fully with an official investigation, right? Ghosh hadn't even searched me or demanded that I surrender my weapons. What could go wrong?

"Rabbit," I said subvocally using the nanos to pick up the tiny impulses I sent to my vocal cords and convert them to speech through my link. "Keep recording. And track us through the station security grid, just in case."

Rabbit sent two electronic clicks through my link to signal he understood. No sense in broadcasting that we were still in communication.

Ghosh's Sergeant was almost as big as Deuce, his bulk further enhanced by a full suit of powered body armor. He looked Tanaka and me up and down before turning and heading toward the airlock at a brisk walk. Tanaka trailed behind me and Ghosh fell in at my right side. The rest of the squad took up station behind and to my left.

"Should I be alarmed or flattered by the size of our escort?" I asked Ghosh as we passed through the personnel lock next to the huge cargo door.

"Akira did say you were a dangerous man," said Ghosh with a shake of his head. "But the 'escort,' as you put it, isn't for you. Two years ago, someone had my partner killed in a fake drug sale. Now, a hired killer is taking shots at his brother. Tanaka and I were never friends, but he is Aki's brother, and I owe it to Aki to keep him safe."

"So the squad is to protect Tanaka?" I asked. "Isn't that a bit much? You could have brought a Fair Witness and a holorecorder to the ship and taken our statements. Even a couple of beat cops could protect Tanaka from anything other than a determined suicide attack if we'd a stayed in the bay, or on my ship."

"But you declined to invite us aboard," Ghosh reminded me with a wry smile.

"I stood on principal because you showed up with a full squad of goons. A polite request would have gotten you and a Fair Witness aboard with nothing stronger than a warning that we were cooperating voluntarily and hadn't agreed to a general search."

He gave me a sidelong look. "You're a funny guy, Mbele. Akira told me you could be a hard-ass about your 'rights.' Why are you so concerned about pushing my official nose in them, and yet willing to cooperate with an investigation?"

I thought about telling him where he could stick his investigation. Going along on the shooting was the path of least resistance and the only way I could find out more about Sayer and why he was dead. Then it occurred to me that this show of force was just that—a show.

"Is that what this is? An investigation?" I asked, nodding toward the giant Sergeant. We were nearing the exit where the cargo terminal jointed the main concourse of the commercial spaceport.

"Meaning what?"

"Meaning, this is a big show of force to collect a couple of cooperating material witnesses. I've seen smaller details escorting heads of state. But, if I wanted to attract attention, this would be a good way to do it. Why are you making Tanaka and me targets?"

"Do you have a reason to feel threatened?" he asked, looking my way but not slackening his pace. "Anything I should know?"

My assessment of Ghosh raised a notch or two. He was clever. If there were others looking for Tanaka, he'd just made it obvious where we were and, by extension, where we could be found later. He had the muscle to ensure they wouldn't make a run at us on the way to the station and, once we were released, he could position men along our route back to *Profit* to report who followed us or take out anyone who tried to hit us. If we made it home safe, no harm done. If he found out who followed us, he had a new lead. If we got killed and his guys took out the assassins, he still won.

"I don't like playing games, Ghosh." I stopped walking and Tanaka stumbled as he tried to avoid walking into me. I faced Ghosh who crossed his arms and glared at me. "And I don't like being bait in someone else's trap. I had enough of that shit back on Mars. I even ran this game myself once or twice. Either arrest us or let us go back to my ship."

Ghosh smiled at me for a second, his expression unreadable. He nodded toward his Sergeant who quickly drew a sidearm and pointed it at my head.

"I didn't want it to come to this," Ghosh said. "Turn around, hands behind your back."

I glanced at the other cops, they had spread out, hands on their weapons as well. Even with nano augmentation, I had no chance of taking them out before one of them shot me down. Tanaka stood very still, his eyes darting from me to the Sergeant to Ghosh and back again.

I shrugged and did as Ghosh had commanded. I had asked for it, after all. He bound my hands with a pair of flexcuffs, and the Sergeant searched me quickly and efficiently. He took my needler and the throwing knife, but left my wallet and passport in the back pocket of my trousers.

"Zachariah Mbele," Ghosh said in flat official tones. "I am placing you under lawful restraint on suspicion of manslaughter in the death of Ian Sayer. You have right to counsel and are cautioned that any statements you make may be recorded as evidence and used against you at trial. You are not required to give any evidence, either knowingly or unknowingly, that may be construed as self-incrimination. You may request that any recorded statements be subjected to judicial review in order to comply with that standard. Do you understand?"

"I understand my rights, Ghosh. This isn't my first orbit. You've got no probable cause. You know that. I'll be out before the charges even get logged."

He smiled as he turned me around. "If you've run this 'game,' as you call it, yourself, then you know it doesn't really matter. Now let's go."

Chapter 3

They separated Tanaka and me when we reached the Spaceport substation. The substation consisted of a central booking room with a front desk and four holomatrix workstations in the front, and six holding cells in the rear in a separate section of the administrative offices near the passenger terminals. The cells were soundproofed, so I couldn't hear Tanaka or communicate with him. I spent a couple of hours napping on the narrow bunk in my cell before Ghosh came for me.

"You're free to go, Mbele," he said without preamble. "The Coroner confirmed that your needles contained only Limbitrol in a non-lethal concentration. The shooting has been ruled legitimate self defense."

"What killed Sayer, then?" I asked as I got to my feet.

"Anectine," he answered. "Injected after he was unconscious. We're looking for the medics who treated him at the scene."

I stopped outside the cell and looked at him. "What do you mean, 'Looking for'?"

He made a face. "They've not checked in with their dispatcher for the past hour."

"And you still think I had something to do with all this?"

"No," he shook his head. "But you're a capable guy. Someone is trying to kill Tanaka Kensai. If you hadn't been at the Imperial today, he'd probably already be dead."

"I called him, looking for his brother. I don't think any hired killer could have known about our meeting in advance." I said. "That means they were watching him and took advantage of an opportunity. I was just in the right place at the right time."

Ghosh nodded and continued. "Someone had Aki killed two years ago. That jolt deal was a trap. At first, I thought it was people connected to the Customs Service because of that big bust he orchestrated based on the information you gave him. But I've got enough contacts in the bureaucracy to know about anyone with enough juice to pull it off. None of those leads panned out. That leaves someone outside of the Highpoint power structure. And now Tanaka's been targeted."

"Who outside of the arcology would care about Akira enough to want him dead?" I asked. "And why go after Tanaka now, two years after Akira's death?"

"I don't know," Ghosh said. "Look, I know you don't like being used as bait, but like I said, you're a capable guy. You can look out for yourself and your people. And Tanaka, if you're willing. The whole purpose of this 'show,' as you called it, was to draw some attention to you. Maybe make them think twice about another run on Tanaka until I can develop some more leads through Sayer and these missing medics."

"I'm a charter boat captain, not a mercenary," I said. "I'm trying to run a legitimate business."

"I'm not asking you to fight," said Ghosh. "Aki told me some things about you; things he learned from the Feds and from some less conventional sources. You've gone up against some powerful enemies and survived. All I'm asking is that you watch out for Tanaka until I can get to the people who want him dead. This is Highpoint. I don't know who I can trust in my own department. Aki trusted

39

you. That's good enough for me."

I should have told him right there that I wanted nothing to do with him or Tanaka or the whole damned arcology. I should have left Tanaka in the holding cells and gone back to the ship and lifted for Tycho as soon as we could get Deuce out of whatever bar he was haunting. But something about that didn't sit right with me. It was too much like running away.

So I nodded to him and said, "Where's Tanaka?"

"In the booking room, waiting for you."

"And if I had told you to stick it where the sun don't shine?"

He shrugged. "I'd have had to find another reason to hold him. At least with you he isn't confined to these holding cells. This is the only station I can be absolutely sure is clean."

"That's a sad situation. Why do you stay if things are that bad?"

He smiled. "It isn't all bad. We catch some of the bad guys and every now and then we get a break, like the one you gave Aki. There are actually more honest cops than not. It's just that the system is broken at the top. I take what small wins I can and keep my head down."

"I have a friend, Henri Boucher, a Captain in the BPS in Tycho City. You should give him a call. He may have some tips for you."

Ghosh nodded thoughtfully. "I may just do that."

I found Tanaka sitting next to the desk Sergeant in the booking room. It was the same big guy who had frisked and then handcuffed me in the docking bay. He now wore a blue Highpoint Security uniform minus the body armor and the same bland expression he'd had before. A consummate professional. He had me sign a voucher and handed me my knife and my needler.

"Are you OK?" I asked Tanaka as I slid the throwing knife into its sheath.

He nodded. "Kamil tells me you've been cleared. He wants me to go back to your ship and stay there for a while."

I nodded and stepped aside to allow a delivery

messenger to hand a package to the desk Sergeant. I slid the needler into its holster.

"Let's get out of here," I said.

Tanaka followed me out through the heavy security doors of the substation and we started across the open concourse toward the freight terminal. We'd only gone a few steps when the delivery messenger came through the doors behind us. I only noticed him because he looked hard at Tanaka and me before turning the opposite way and breaking into a run.

Time seemed to slow as the nanos sped up my reaction time and heightened my senses. I pushed Tanaka to the deck and drew the needler. The messenger ran straight away from the substation, shoving people out of his way. "Stop!" I shouted as I leveled the needler.

The explosion knocked me off my feet before I could take the shot. The heavy security doors of the station flew over my head, as I lay dazed on the deck. Smoke and flame poured out of the substation. Somewhere an alarm whooped and people started screaming.

I shook my head, trying to clear it and got to my knees. The messenger was gone. People ran about in confusion as clouds of fire suppressant jetted from the overhead. I looked toward the substation, but there was no sign of anyone coming out. The interior was still an inferno, despite the clouds of suppressant.

I stood and hauled Tanaka to his feet and shoved him toward the freight terminal. "Go," I shouted. I took one last, hopeless look at the substation before following him.

Cleo stood in the forward cargo hold, waiting for us as we stepped in through the sally port. "What happened, Zack? Eddie saw a huge flash on the security monitors, then the view shifted to the main concourse. The substation is burning."

"A bomb," I said. "A messenger brought a package in just as Tanaka and I were leaving. Ghosh cut us loose. The hit man I shot at the Imperial was injected with Anectine sometime after my needles put him out." I turned to Tanaka. "Go up to the salon. Wait up there. Tell Rabbit I'll want to talk with him about these files of

Akira's so have him upload them to Sylvia. Got it?"

Tanaka nodded and wisely kept his mouth shut as he slouched toward the ladder.

Cleo leaned in close to me and asked, "What is he doing here? I thought he was Ghosh's problem."

"Ghosh is dead. The bomb took out the whole substation and everyone in it. It was meant for Tanaka, and maybe me as well. Just before he turned me loose, Ghosh asked me to keep Tanaka under wraps until he could find out more about who wants to kill him. Ghosh didn't trust anyone in his department other than his personal team and didn't want to risk protective custody."

"What the hell, Zack?" said Cleo. "We're a charter business, not a babysitting service. Let the Highpoint cops deal with this."

"I sort of gave my word," I said. "Besides, whoever did this has the juice and the nerve to hit a police substation just to get at Tanaka. He won't be safe anywhere the Highpoint cops stash him."

"And it's so much safer aboard the ship? What's to keep these people, whoever they are, from blowing up the *Profit*, too? This is our home, Zack. We can't take this kind of risk."

"I promised Ghosh I'd look after Tanaka," I repeated.

"Ghosh is dead. No one expects you to keep a promise to a dead man."

I shook my head. "Those are just the sorts of promises you have to keep." I held up a hand as she started to speak again. "I know it's risky, and I should have asked first. But in the end, all we have is our reputation. In the past, that meant we did the job, no matter what, and we got paid. That hasn't changed just because we hire out to rich folks who want a private yacht for a while. We do the job we contract for and we get paid. The money is nice, but all we really have is our reputation. How will it look if a tough bunch of ex-pirates backs out of a promise just because it might be dangerous to keep it?"

"Just who's supposed to pay us here? The Highpoint authorities? Tanaka?"

I took her arm and guided her toward the ladder to

the upper deck. "I intend to find that out. There's more to Tanaka's story than he's told us so far."

Rabbit and Tanaka were waiting for us in the salon. Tanaka had managed to find the bar and had a drink in his hand. The way it shook, I figured he needed it and didn't begrudge him a shot or two.

Cleo had other ideas. She didn't speak to him but crossed the salon, closed the cover on the liquor cabinet and locked it. Then she pointed to one of the armchairs. Tanaka sat down like a guilty child.

"Rabbit," I said, "did Tanaka give you Akira's files?"

"Sylvia already has them, Zack. I glanced over them. There are a lot of references to Ceres and to glowgems in general, but nothing that we didn't already have from the stuff you gave his brother three years ago."

"How about the security feeds from the substation," I said. "Any idea who sent that bomb?"

"The feed went blank as soon as the bomb went off. I wasn't watching that screen after you and Tanaka left. Do you want me to check the image between then and the time of the explosion?"

I nodded. It seemed clear to me that the messenger had delivered the bomb, but why would anyone risk sending it through a delivery service? They'd have to be watching the same security feed Rabbit had tapped into in order to set it off at the right time. Except, if it was intended for Tanaka, then they'd missed the timing by a few seconds. Then I remembered the queer look the messenger had given me and Tanaka before he took off running. He'd known.

"Rabbit," I said. "Look at the delivery guy. Run his image through face recognition. See of the system knows who he was. See if there are any logos on his clothing we can use to track the delivery service and find him."

"Already on it, Zack. I can cross reference with the Federal database, too, if I use the Highpoint security account. I already have an administrators pass for that. Set it up three years ago with a regular renewal macro that..." Rabbit prattled on in slicer babble for a while as he flipped through the security images at half second intervals.

He stopped in mid-sentence as a file popped up in his matrix. It showed a head and shoulders hologram of a dark-haired man with deep-set almond shaped eyes and a bland expression. I recognized the face of the delivery messenger.

"Holy shit," said Rabbit. The lines of text next to the image identified him as Kim Song Rhee, thirty-seven years old, a native of Planetia, Mars. Former service in the Martian Penal System at Brunault Prison, delta block. Currently employed as a security consultant for Kwai Hong Holdings.

My nanos twitched at the thought of the Bear, Brunault Prison. Delta block had been for ordinary criminals, not political *lechs* like Rabbit and me. Alpha block had been our own special hell for nearly two years under the tender care of guards like Jed Clancy. I shuddered. Clancy was dead by my own hand, but that didn't stop the momentary panic that welled up in me at the thought of that place.

I shook myself back to reality and forced the nanos back into their resting state. This wasn't about the Bear. This was about Kwai Hong. Something about Akira Kensai's files was important to him.

"What do you know about purging Federal databases, Rabbit? Are they clean wipes all over the system, or could copies remain? What I want to know is whether a file that was on the secure Federal server on Ceres before the Kwai's took over could still be there."

Rabbit thought for a second, surprised by the sudden change in subject. "Sure it's possible. But it's more likely the files were purged when the base was sold to old man Kwai. Do you think that's why he sent this guy after you?"

Tanaka spoke up. "No, they weren't. Akira told me that was part of the deal. The Federal server contained all of the life support specs, plus the mining survey data. The base was old and the life support systems were custom designs, not modular like modern systems. Leaving the files was part of the deal. The Feds purged any sensitive data and left the rest."

"Could you slice those files and find out what's in

them?" I asked Rabbit.

He shrugged. "No problem, if I can access the server. But shit, Zack, to do that we'd have to go to Ceres. We can't go there. Kwai Hong wants you dead. He's just made that pretty clear."

"Just asking," I said. "So far, I haven't heard anything that makes going there worth my while."

"I didn't say anything about going after the files," protested Tanaka.

"Bullshit," I said. "Curiosity about some old files doesn't get you killed. Not unless there's money in it. You hinted you wanted somebody who was willing to break rules. What rules?"

Tanaka wouldn't meet my eye. "It's just an expression. I meant someone who wouldn't mind prying into a Fed database to get Malloy's report."

"The Feds wouldn't hire a hitman to kill you. They'd send a special ops team to pick you up and you'd just disappear." I moved in front of him and forced him to meet my eye. "Kwai Hong sent a paid assassin after you. When that failed he made sure the gunman wouldn't talk and then sent his own people to take out any witnesses. Ghosh wasn't on their payroll and, when he got me involved, they didn't hesitate to take him out. Kwai expended a lot of juice and went to a lot of trouble to do that. Why does he want you dead?"

"I don't know for sure," he said. "Maybe he's after you."

I slammed my hand on the table. "No more crap. Why does he want to kill you?"

"He wants Akira's notes." Tanaka slumped in the chair. "A couple of months ago someone from Kwai Hong Holdings offered me two thousand yuan for all of Akira's glowgem files. I said no. I figured if they wanted them that badly, there must be something important in the missing report, something worth more than they offered."

"Can't see old man Kwai wanting to kill you over that."

"It didn't end there," said Tanaka. "I used to be in banking. I called in some favors and used a few trading databases and started to look into the glowgem business. There are only a handful of companies making them these days. The profit margin is slim and the market's fickle. In the last few months, Kwai Hong Holdings has bought up all but one of them."

I shrugged. "Sounds like Kwai's trying to corner the market. That's not illegal."

Tanaka shook his head. "It's not that simple. When he buys the companies, he liquidates them. Sometimes at a loss. Whatever he's after, it isn't control of the glowgem market."

"What company hasn't he bought yet?"

"Rainbow Gems."

"Sylvia," I called. "What have you got on Rainbow Gems?"

"Searching," she said in that computer voice she used when she was crunching data. "Started by a pair of chemical techs from Nucor about three years ago, just after the glowgem files went public. Did well as one of the first to market synthetic gems. About six months after their initial launch, Nucor bought them out and took over gem production. Made the original partners a boatload of cash."

"What's Nucor's position in Rainbow?" Rabbit asked.

"Nucor owns them outright. They're the major revenue generator for the parent company since the demand for biochips tanked."

"So Nucor isn't likely to sell out," I said. "I don't see why Kwai Hong is so interested in glowgems, but he doesn't do anything unless there's money in it."

"Whatever it is, it has something to do with that report," Tanaka said. "First they offered me the cash. Then they sent a couple of guys in expensive suits to tell me to stop looking into Kwai Hong's business. I tried to negotiate with them, but they said the time for negotiations was past. Then they tried to have me killed."

I had to agree with him. I wasn't about to tell him that, but it made sense. Why else would Kwai care about Akira Kensai's notes? I looked Tanaka over again. He was dressed in a well-cut business suit but there were a couple of faint stains on the lapels that had obviously resisted several attempts at cleaning, and the cuffs of his shirt were slightly frayed. His shoes were polished to a high shine, but the heels were heavily worn down.

"Why didn't you take the cash?" I asked. "Looks like you could use it. Why put yourself in Kwai Hong's way?"

His face darkened. "What do you mean, I could use it."

"I've seen better suits in the second-hand stalls around Freetown, and you drink like a man who's been down to the bottom of more than one bottle. You're down on your luck and you think this file is your winning ticket."

He looked away and didn't answer me.

Cleo stood and walked over to him. She placed a hand on each arm of his chair and leaned in close to his face. "He asked you a question," she said quietly. Her voice was soft, almost gentle, but her eyes were as cold as a lunar night. "Zack has given his word to protect you. I know him well. He won't do anything to hurt you or allow anyone outside of this ship to harm you. But he doesn't speak for me. I am half owner of this ship. This is as much my home and my business as it is Zack's. Now, I want you to answer his questions and tell us everything we need to know or I'll . . ." She whispered something in his ear that I couldn't hear, even with my nanos. Tanaka went pale and swallowed hard. Cleo reached up and stroked his cheek with the back of her hand. He flinched as if she'd burned him with her touch. She stood and walked past me and out of the salon.

Tanaka followed her with his eyes until she turned down the passageway to our quarters. He kept his eyes fixed there for a few seconds as he started talking.

"Like I said," he began. "I was in banking. Investments and asset management. There were some irregularities with a few client accounts. No losses, mind you, just some unusual fund transfers that came back to me. No one lost any money. I made sure of that."

"You used other peoples funds for your own investments and hoped to pay it back from the profits." I said.

He nodded. "Except the investments didn't pay out fast enough. I used every yuan I had to cover the shortage." He finally looked at me, salvaging some dignity. "No one lost any money because of me."

"But they fired you anyway."

He nodded. "I've been doing some accounting, odd jobs, but no one will hire me. I thought of leaving Highpoint, maybe for Tycho or Tharsis, someplace where my background wouldn't be as important. But travel costs money. When Kwai's people approached me, I saw a chance. Two thousand was a decent offer, but it wouldn't be enough to pay off the debts I've run up in the past year and still have enough to start over. I just wanted a little more. Five thousand would have covered everything."

"Anything more?"

He shook his head. "No. Honestly. I just wanted a fair price. I figured they'd haggle and bluster a bit, but what's five thousand yuan to a man like Kwai Hong?"

I thought about that. Five thousand was throw away money to Kwai Hong. Not worth a second thought. Certainly not a killing amount. Unless it wasn't about the money, or Akira's files.

"You said the two goons who braced you didn't ask for the files?"

"No," Tanaka said. "They told me to stay out of Kwai Hong's business. I wasn't sure what they meant by that. All I wanted was to negotiate with him."

"This was after you started asking your contacts about the glowgem market, right?"

He nodded. "Is that what they were talking about? But there's nothing illegal in what Kwai is doing. It doesn't make good business sense, but it isn't illegal."

I didn't get it either, but the dynamic clearly had changed once Tanaka started investigating the gem market. Kwai was up to something. It had something to do with the glowgem market and it was big enough to kill for. And now I was in it too, whether I liked it or not. Word would get back to Kwai Hong that Tanaka was with me. The opportunity to kill two birds with one stone would be too good for him to pass up. We needed to find out what was so important about that purged report if we wanted to stay alive.

"Rabbit, are you sure you can slice that database?" I asked.

"If the file's there, I can find it," he said. "But, Zack, it's Ceres. How are we gonna get in there?"

"Bigger question is, how am I going to sell it to Cleo?"

I had Rabbit escort Tanaka to a cabin while I went forward to the cockpit.

"Sylvia, I need to talk to Sam Guthrie. Can you track him down?"

"Sure, Zack. He's registered at the Imperial, same place you went to meet Tanaka Kensai. Why? He's booked for a two-week stay and I don't think Cleo plans to stick around that long."

"Just get him," I said.

It took less time than I expected. Guys like Guthrie usually had layers of secretaries between themselves and unsolicited calls. Guthrie answered the call himself.

"Mr. Guthrie, Zack Mbele here. Thank you for speaking with me."

"Cut the crap, Mbele," he said, a hint of amusement in his voice. "What do you want?"

"I was wondering if you did business with Kwai Hong? Specifically, do you buy ice from him?"

"Yeah, I deal with the old bastard. Charges twice the prices on Mars because he knows he's the only game in town if you want to sell water in the Belt. Shipping costs from Mars or Earth are too high to make a profit, so all roads to the Belt go through Ceres." His eyes narrowed. "I hear he's got it in for you. Wants you dead. Why are you asking about him?"

"I need to go to Ceres." I outlined the story of Kensai's files, Tanaka's brush with the assassin and the link to Malloy's report in the old Ceres database. "I have a data slicer who can retrieve the report, but he needs access to the Ceres server."

"Is Conejo that good?" He must have noticed my surprise because he smiled. "Yeah, I checked you out. You're the real deal. I wouldn't have figured a guy like you for a charter boat captain." The smile faded. "But then, most of my old squad mates wouldn't see me selling ice."

"Can you get me docking clearance for Ceres?"

"I can do better than that. I can charter your ship to

take me there."

"Why would you do that?" I asked. "Kwai Hong wants me dead. I have good reason to believe he's behind the guy who made a run at us in the lobby bar and that he killed both the shooter and the medics who juiced him up with Anectine. On top of that, he blew up a police substation because he thought Tanaka was being held there. He's a dangerous man and he won't think twice about killing me or anyone on my ship.

He shrugged. "My wife and step-daughter can find plenty of entertainment here. Unless I want to go shopping with them, I have nothing to do but drink in the hotel bar. I do enough business with Kwai to make an excuse to meet him on Ceres. That'll get you in without any questions. Not like I haven't had to chat with him about a light shipment before." I shook my head, but he held up a hand. "I'm prominent enough that he'll think twice about going after your ship with me on it. It'll get you in the door. Once you're on Ceres he may be able to separate us, so you'll have to be very careful there. Let me do this. It'll be worth it to stick it to Kwai."

I couldn't come up with a better idea, so I agreed. Besides, it would make it easier to sell the trip to Cleo.

Chapter 4

As expected, Cleo balked.

"You can't be serious," she said. "I thought we were past this sort of bullshit. You have responsibilities now. You can't put everything we've built at risk because you want to go back to playing pirate."

"First," I said, my voice cold. "I never played. I always took what we did seriously. Second, I gave Ghosh my word. Now, I could throw Tanaka out and no one would be the wiser. No one but me. Would you really have stayed with me if I didn't do what I said I'd do? If I'd have taken the safe and secure path back when we first met? I haven't grown so 'respectable' that things like a promise to a man I respected have less meaning than making a few yuan. Finally, if we can get something on Kwai, it may give us leverage to make him leave us alone. Something in Tanaka's information or in those files on Ceres is worth killing for. I aim to find out what it is."

"And what about me? Don't I get some say in what we do with the ship and the business?" she asked.

"This will be business," I said. "Sam Guthrie is chartering us to take him to Ceres. As far as Kwai Hong will know, it's a legitimate business deal."

"What possible reason would Sam Guthrie have for visiting Ceres?"

"He's sells ice all over the system. Ceres is the only known source between Mars and the rings of Saturn. Sam's whole operation in the Belt is based on Ceres ice. He found out Kwai's shipments are light and wants a meeting. Who better to take him there for a quick turn around than us?"

Cleo shook her head. "You'll never get him to go along with that."

"He already has," I said. "It was his idea."

"Then I don't know who is crazier," she said. "You or him."

In the end, it took a call to Guthrie to convince her that he was serious about the charter. Even then, he'd had to guarantee a bond worth the value of the ship before she agreed. I told Sylvia to track Deuce down on his link and have him get back to the ship. I wanted to lift as soon as Guthrie was aboard.

Guthrie arrived less than an hour later. He traveled light with only a suit bag slung over his shoulder and a small valise in his hand.

He caught my look and smiled. "I was an infantry officer in the War. Learned to travel light and fast."

Deuce showed up a few minutes after Guthrie, looking surly and walking with a slight hunch in his shoulders. He only grunted in response to my greeting. I put it down to his being angry at having his leave interrupted on short notice. He disappeared into his workshop before I could explain.

The trip out to the Belt was uneventful. Cleo was a charming hostess, as usual, and Guthrie seemed happier without his wife and stepdaughter. He even sought out Deuce and the two of them shared a drink in Deuce's workshop. After that, Deuce seemed to return to his usual taciturn self.

Kwai Hong's security crew wasn't exactly friendly, but they didn't give us more than a cursory inspection when we docked at Ceres. Guthrie was right. As long as we were with him, Kwai wasn't going to make a run at us. Money trumped personal revenge with the old man. Still, I restricted everyone to the ship until we were ready to make our move.

We gathered on the main deck an hour after docking. Guthrie had made an appointment to see Kwai Hong and Deuce, Rabbit and I were gearing up to slice the Ceres database. Tanaka was in a guest cabin and would wait for us there. Cleo wore a light grey business suit and carried a small datapad. She would go with Guthrie as his personal assistant.

"I don't need help," Guthrie said.

"No," I replied. "But I won't be responsible for you getting hurt. Cleo will make sure you get back to the ship."

"No offense, Cleo," Githrie said. "But they won't let us near Kwai Hong armed."

"I know," she said with a sweet smile. I almost laughed. Cleo was the best unarmed fighter I'd ever seen. In a standup fight, no weapons, she could take Deuce. Maybe even me, if I didn't use my nanos. Guthrie would be safe.

"How did you get Kwai to see you?" I asked.

"I told him I was tired of my shipments being shorted. He protested, but not too strenuously because it's true. I demanded to renegotiate our contract. He'll try to stonewall me into giving in." Guthrie shrugged. "It's business. Something I understand."

"How much time will you need to slice the file?" asked Cleo.

"A few minutes, maybe. No more than an hour," Rabbit said.

Cleo looked at Guthrie. He nodded. "No problem," he said. "Kwai likes to pretend he's old school Chinese. We'll have tea and a light meal before he'll discuss business"

Guthrie and Cleo left arm in arm. I gave them ten minutes before we headed out. Deuce asked the security guard at the docking bay lock where we could get a drink. He directed us to an employee bar on the second deck. We thanked him and headed to the lifts.

On the second deck the lift opened into a long narrow passageway. Several compartments opened off of it, all vacant. We ducked into the third one and Rabbit rolled over to an access panel on the wall. He unscrewed the panel and began sorting through the relays and cable leads behind it. Deuce and I watched the door, needlers ready. We were packing sleepers; most of Kwai's people were just employees, working folk doing a job. No need for killing here.

A few seconds later, Rabbit activated his virtual keyboard and began fingering away. "Well, that was easy," he said after a minute or so.

I turned to look at him. "What have you got?"

"Malloy's report," said Rabbit.

"You're sure?"

"It's got a Fed tracking code, the right date, and his ID number. It's his all right. I figured Kwai might have found it so I checked his personal database first. You'd think a big shot like him would be more savvy about file security. He didn't even encrypt it. And he has a ridiculously obvious password."

"Rabbit, enough," I interrupted. "Upload the file to Sylvia and let's get out of here."

"Done."

Deuce scanned the outer corridor, then nodded. The file was safe with Sylvia, so as long as we weren't in a restricted area, there was no reason for stealth. We strolled down the passageway to the bar the security man had suggested and ordered some beers. We had time to finish our drinks before Kim Song Rhee showed up with a squad of security goons.

My nanofibers kicked in, and I started to reach for my needler. The whine of a pulse rifle charging up next to my head made me think better of it. I looked at Deuce and shook my head. He placed his hands carefully on the table and glared at Kim.

The security guards stood us up one by one and frisked us. They took our needlers, my boot knife and Deuce's backup pneumatic. Kim stood expectantly over Rabbit until he drew a slim pneumatic from a compartment in the arm of his chair and set it on the table. One of the security guards took it and stood back from the table.

The rest of the squad cleared the bar, quickly and efficiently but with an attitude that implied no resistance would be tolerated. Two minutes later, a hatch behind the bar opened and Kwai Hong himself stepped into the compartment.

"Welcome to Ceres, Mr. Mbele," Kwai said pleasantly. "You, too, Mr. Conejo. Although, I would have thought a slicer as talented as you would detect a data trap when he encountered one."

Rabbit grimaced. "Sorry, Zack," he said to me. "There must have been a trap on the file that set off an alarm when I accessed it. Stupid mistake."

"No problem, Rabbit," I said. "I'm sure Mr. Kwai means us no harm. We're here on a legitimate charter. Isn't that right, Kwai?" I was reminding him that Sam Guthrie was too important to just disappear and we were under his protection.

Kwai smiled the same cold smile his son had used as he was preparing to turn me into human sushi. "Of course. Mr. Guthrie and Ms. Lee are in my office. Tanaka Kensai will be with them shortly. Shall we join them?"

It wasn't a request. The security guys kept us covered with pulse rifles as we followed Kwai to a lift. A few minutes later, we arrived at his office. Most of the Ceres installation was underground. Above ground radiation and particle shielding is expensive. Kwai's office flaunted expense with a huge transparent window high above the asteroid's surface with views of the landing docks and smelter mirrors.

Cleo and Guthrie stood near the window. Tanaka sat in a chair nearby, looking frightened. No one seemed surprised to see us.

"What's going on, Kwai?" asked Guthrie. "We're here to do business, not play vendetta."

"No one will be harmed. At least, not here and now," said Kwai. "I want you to witness a demonstration, after which, you are free to go."

"What sort of demonstration?"

Kwai smiled his crocodile smile. "All in good time. I'd intended to delay this for another week, but Mr. Kensai's intransigence forced my hand." Tanaka shifted nervously in his chair. "Had he taken the money, this inconvenience would not be necessary."

"Inconvenience," I repeated. "That's what you call the deaths of Ian Sayer, the two medics and at least a dozen Highpoint Security officers? Kamil Ghosh was a good cop. Why wait two years after killing Akira Kensai to go after his partner?"

Kwai's smile never wavered. "As I said, if Mr. Kensai had been more sensible than his brother, none of that would have been necessary."

"You had Aki killed?" Tanaka asked, only now beginning to see the pattern.

Kwai barely glanced at him before returning his gaze to me. "Once I realized what Akira Kensai was looking for, it didn't take long to find it in the old Federal database. The implications were...disturbing. I couldn't allow that information to be made public in the same way he had revealed the secret of culturing glowgems."

"But the culture technique was already public knowledge." Tanaka sputtered. "You didn't have to kill Aki over that."

"Why are you buying up glowgem companies?" I asked, ignoring Tanaka. "Your operations never included gems."

"Very good, Mr. Mbele," Kwai said. "You see to the heart of the matter. I have no interest in gems, only in the company that makes them."

"Nucor," said Guthrie. "You're making a run at Nucor."

"Why?" I asked. "If he's not interested in gems, why Nucor?"

Kwai said nothing, only looked at Guthrie expectantly.

"Ice. It's about the ice. Nucor holds title to a third of the ice on Ceres."

Kwai nodded. "And once I buy out Nucor, I will own it all and be able to set the market price in the Belt."

"But how does shutting down Nucor's competition help you?" I asked. "By creating a shortage of gems, you've increased their profits."

"I've made them more dependent on the gem market," Kwai said. "Now please turn to the window and watch."

I looked and now could see a small smelter vessel moving into position at the focal point of the big mirrors. It stopped and the mirrors began to move. Sunlight focused onto the center of the smelter crucible and it began to glow red. Suddenly, a new light shone from the crucible, brilliant white at the center of the dull red. The light was blinding. In response, the window darkened. My eyes adjusted and I gasped.

The bright light expanded and thinned, like a glowing membrane. It grew until it dwarfed the crucible, and then began to fade from eye searing brilliance to mere bright glow. I could make out detail through the light; spoke-like structures linked by glowing membranes. Then it began to move.

"It's alive," whispered Cleo.

The structure, creature, whatever it was undulated slowly away from the smelter and began to move past the window, heading outward toward the black beyond the Belt.

Kwai spoke softly as we watched the thing move slowly away from us. "Malloy found them. He worked out their life cycle. Glowgems are their larvae. They drift through the Belt for thousands of years accumulating silicates. Then they hitch a ride on a passing comet as it falls inward to the sun. When the gems are heated to nine hundred degrees Celsius, they transform into adults and ride the solar wind out to the Oort cloud where the cycle starts again."

"Glowgems are alive?" asked Tanaka.

"Natural ones are," said Kwai. "Cultured gems glow at body temperatures but are infertile. They can't become adults."

"You're going to make this public," I said. "The Feds will call a moratorium on gem sales. They won't risk another fiasco like the Martian virus scare. This is the first documentation of extraterrestrial life, and they can't allow half the population to walk around wearing an alien life form as jewelry."

Kwai nodded, his smile smug. "The gem market will crash and Nucor will be more than willing to accept my buyout offer of twice their current price per share. By the time it's revealed that cultured gems aren't alive, it will be too late for Nucor."

We watched in silence until the gossamer creature was out of sight. Then Kwai waved to the security guards and they herded us all to the lift. Kwai said good-bye, all polite and proper, but the look in his eyes told me that things would be very different the next time we met.

We were escorted back to the *Profit* and cleared for launch. The mood aboard ship was somber. Guthrie had renegotiated his ice contract on very favorable terms that were locked in for at least two years, but even he seemed to feel that we'd been beaten somehow. As I left the cockpit after clearing the Ceres zone of control, I heard Cleo whistling happily from our quarters.

"What are you so happy about," I asked as I entered and flopped down on our bed.

"You should kiss me because I'm such a smart businesswoman," she said.

"I'll gladly kiss you, anytime. But what did you do that makes you so smart?"

"Well, on the way out, I talked with Sam about the ice business. I figured that whatever Kwai had up his sleeve, it had something to do with Nucor and the gems. But when Sam told me that Nucor held the title on a lot of ice on Ceres, I started to see an opportunity. So I bought as many shares of Nucor as I could with our charter fee."

I sat up on the bed. "How many shares?"

"At five yuan and change per share, a little less than a thousand. When they sell to Kwai Hong at double the list price, it should net us a very respectable profit."

Then I did kiss her, long and slow.

FROM
CERES WITH
LOVE

The hologram caught Deuce's eye as he passed the club. He stopped and watched the miniature figure for a long moment. She hadn't changed; petite, almost doll-like with pale skin and hair that was salt white except for a single lock of violet sweeping from the right side of her forehead to her shoulder. Her eyes were violet as well; bright and gleaming like the amethyst pendant that hung between her small breasts. Deuce smiled. *'Grace Tyler, two sets nightly 20:00 and 22:00'* read the marquee above the hologram.

The door to the club was open and Deuce looked in. A cleaning 'bot hummed across the floor. Chairs were stacked upside down on the tables and the lights behind the bar were bright enough to show the dust on the more expensive liquor bottles. A piano played softly from the bandstand. Deuce couldn't see who was playing, but the tune sounded familiar. He stepped closer.

"Who's there?" a woman called from behind the piano.

"I thought I recognized that tune," Deuce said, stepping up onto the bandstand.

Grace stood and walked toward him. She felt the edge of the piano and held a hand out to him, her sightless eyes looking directly at him as if she could see him. She always did that. It still unnerved him.

"Sven," she said as her fingers touched his. "I didn't know you were on Highpoint."

"I just got in," he said taking her tiny hand in his. "We had a charter..."

She slammed her knee into his crotch and he doubled over. Her fist smashed into his right ear and he sprawled on the floor.

"That's for leaving me on Delilah, you son of a bitch."

Deuce rubbed his ear as he turned over to a sitting position. "I asked you to wait for me. I came back for you, but you weren't there."

"You have to give a girl a better reason than 'I've got to go to Mars and pick up my old Lieutenant. I'll be back in a few months.' What was I supposed to do in the meantime?"

"Zack needed me." Deuce gently shifted his weight to ease the ache between his legs.

She dropped down on the floor beside him, leaning her head on his arm and holding his hand. "I needed you."

Deuce put his arms around her and pulled her close. She felt tiny and vulnerable in his arms and, as always, he worried he would crush her. She stiffened at first, then melted into his embrace and he felt like he had that first time, in a club on Ceres.

***

The bar wasn't the kind of place Deuce usually went for a drink. Too upscale for his taste with small tables lit by tiny glow globes that hardly shed enough light to see the tabletop, much less read the fancy menu the waiter shoved under his nose. But the only other choice on Ceres was the bar at the employee recreation center and that was full of off-duty Feddies. Even though he was under a termination order back on Mars, he still considered himself a Sergeant in the Martian Special Forces. Drinking in the same bar with a bunch of Federal grunts didn't seem like a good idea to him.

He set the menu on the table and grabbed the waiter's sleeve before he could get away. "Beer," Deuce said. "Whatever you have on draft."

The waiter hurried away and Deuce shifted in the chair so he could see the door and the stage at the same time. He didn't think the Martian Third Directorate would make a run at him here, but he believed in being cautious. The war between Mars and the Federation of Earth and the Moon was winding down and Ceres was officially neutral territory, but covert attacks from both sides still happened.

He scanned the room slowly. Most of the patrons were better dressed than he was, a mixture of business suits and casual chic that spelled money. The bar seemed to cater to the travelers who came to Ceres to do business with the big corporations that ran the place. Employees, workers and ship's crew did their drinking in the canteens on the lower decks.

His beer arrived and he drank it slowly. At the prices this place charged, he'd have to make it last. It was good beer, though. Real stout, probably imported from Earth. He eased back into the chair and savored the thick malty taste.

The lights dimmed slightly and a spotlight illuminated the small stage about a meter and a half to his left. Somewhere a piano began playing. Deuce recognized the song: "Red Sand," an old Martian blues ballad.

"Ladies and Gentlemen," said a voice over the sound of the piano. "Ms. Grace Tyler."

A small, slim figure stepped out of the shadows and into the spotlight amidst a smattering of polite applause. Deuce took a deep swallow of his beer before setting the glass carefully on the table. He realized he was staring but no longer cared.

She wasn't the most beautiful woman he'd ever seen, but something about the way she moved into the spotlight and began to sing the old song touched him. Her voice reached inside of him and tugged at feelings he hadn't known he possessed. He knew the words, had known them from the time he was a child but somehow they sounded new when she sang them. She finished the last verse, ending on a high, pure note that she held for an impossibly long time. As Deuce joined in the applause that swelled as the song ended, he realized there were tears coursing down his cheeks. He wiped his eyes and gulped the last of his beer as the piano began playing again and she started another number.

He lost track of time somewhere in the middle of the third song. All he heard was her voice; all he saw was her strange violet eyes. The set ended and she left the stage. Deuce switched from beer to bourbon during the intermission, no longer caring what it cost.

The second set was even more captivating than the first. The songs ranged from smoky torch songs to upbeat love ballads. Deuce couldn't have named a single one, but her voice was indelibly burned into his heart and his brain. The set finished and he rose to his feet, clapping along with the applause that filled the small space.

Grace bowed several times, then turned to the back of the stage and gestured into the shadows. The lights came up and revealed a piano. A slim man with long black hair drawn back in a pony tail stood up from the keyboard and bowed shyly before sitting quickly down. The spotlight cut out and the room lights brightened a bit. Recorded music played softly from the ceiling and Grace stepped toward the table where Deuce sat.

She descended the single step from the stage to the floor and walked to his table. An outstretched hand brushed the tabletop and she stopped, placing her left hand flat on it and extending the right hand toward him. Something about the way she stood was odd. She was facing him, but not directly.

"I'm Grace Tyler," she said. "Thank you for your enthusiastic applause."

Deuce reached out his hand to shake hers, but when she didn't move to meet his grasp he looked more closely at her. She seemed to be looking right at him, but her eyes were not focused on his. They seemed to be looking at his right shoulder. He grasped her hand and she immediately adjusted her stance to face him more squarely. *She's blind,"* he thought.

"You have a great voice," he said with a slight stammer.

She laughed. "It's adequate," she said. "You're new here. What's your name?"

"Deuce Gulbrandsen," he said.

She laughed again. "Deuce? Isn't that some kind of playing card? What was your mother thinking?"

Deuce frowned. "Actually, my name's Sven. Sven Gulbrandsen the second. Never liked the name, so, Deuce."

"I like Sven. It's a strong name. You should be proud of it."

Deuce shrugged, then blushed as he realized she couldn't see the gesture. She smiled and sat down in the chair opposite his, her faced turned toward him, her eyes looking his way. It unnerved him slightly when her face followed him as he shifted in his chair.

"How do you do that?" he asked.

"Do what?"

"Follow me like that. I mean, I know you can't see me, but you look right at me."

She smiled. "My secret. Does it bother you? Should I wear dark glasses and stare at the wall?"

"No," Deuce said quickly. "No offense, just curious, that's all." He looked at the tabletop. This was going the way it usually did when he talked to women. At least the pretty ones.

She reached across the table and touched his hand. "It's all right, Sven. I'm not offended. It surprises a lot of people."

"Yes, ma'am," he said.

"It's Grace." She raised her hand as the waiter passed. Deuce wondered how she knew who it was, but the waiter didn't seem surprised. "Another drink, please, Henry. What are you drinking, Sven?"

"Bourbon," said Deuce. He didn't like the sly smile on the waiter's face but didn't want to start any trouble.

"Bring me one, too, please," Grace said. "And be nice, Henry. Deuce is a friend of mine." That seemed to surprise the waiter, and he hurried away. Deuce smiled. Serves him right, he thought.

"So what brings you to Ceres?" Grace asked. "You don't seem the type to drink in overpriced clubs like this one."

"I'm a miner. My brother and I run a small survey business. We did some work for Ceres Mining on the outer 'roids. Came here to get paid."

"So, you decided to splurge and see my show?" she teased.

"No. I mean, I liked the show and all, but the employee canteen is more my speed."

"And yet you're here."

Deuce sighed. "The canteen didn't seem too friendly, at least not to me."

She frowned. "The garrison troops, you mean. I can't imagine that they'd intimidate a man like you."

"Before I went into business with Mike, that's my brother, I did some time in the Martian military. Don't seem right to me to drink with Feddies. No need to go looking for trouble."

"The war has forced a lot of people to take sides. Despite Colonel Metternich's methods, Mars has many friends in the Belt, even if Ceres is maintaining an illusion of neutrality."

"Metternich ain't Mars," Deuce said bitterly. The waiter returned with their drinks. Deuce took a sip.

Grace lifted her glass. "To Mars," she said, then drank it down and slammed the empty glass down onto the table.

Deuce gulped. "You drink like a miner."

"I wasn't always a famous torch singer." She held up the glass and Henry rushed over to take it from her. "Again, please, Henry."

Deuce finished his more slowly. He was several drinks ahead of her and didn't want to ruin the night by getting drunk or running out of cash.

He needn't have worried. Grace sipped the next drink as they talked about her singing. She'd been on Ceres for a few months, signed to a six month contract by Kwai Hong Holdings, the conglomerate that owned the bar and about half of the asteroid as well.

"Kwai Li Fan manages the club," she said. "He's Kwai Hong's oldest son but doesn't seem to have his father's head for business. I think the old man lets him run this place so he can keep an eye on him. Li is sweet but not too bright."

"He a good friend of yours?" asked Deuce carefully.

She laughed. "You mean am I sleeping with him? No. Not that he hasn't suggested it."

"You must have a lot of guys sweet on you."

"Some," she said with a cock of her head. "Most are transients; businessmen looking for a quick fling before going home to their wives. Henry over there is horribly jealous of you right now." Deuce glanced at the waiter who was watching them intently. "Li has had him escorting me to my rooms every night since I started here, just to make sure I get there safely. He's developed quite a crush on me."

"So, why's he jealous of me?"

"Because you're going to take me home tonight."

Deuce swallowed the rest of his bourbon and fought down the feeling that he was in way over his head. "Yes, Ma'am," he said.

She stood and reached a hand toward him. He nearly upset the table as he stood up. She smiled. Deuce thumbed the payment pad in the center of the table and was surprised to find that the bill had been paid. He frowned.

"Not sure I like a girl paying my tab," he said.

"Not to worry. I won't tell a soul."

"How do we do this?" he asked.

"I take your arm and we walk. I know the way. I just need you to make sure I don't trip over anything or walk into someone else in the passageway. Call it vanity, but a stick or cane doesn't make much of a fashion statement."

Deuce laughed at that. "And a tunnel rat like me does?"

"Perhaps." She reached up and passed her hand over his face, her fingertips brushing the contours of it. "You have a strong jaw, a well formed face. Your nose has been broken, but it gives your face character. Yes, I think I'll look good on your arm. Shall we?"

She nestled her arm into the crook of his elbow and they walked past the bar and out into the passageway. She directed him through a series of corridors until they came to a warren of comfortable apartments. Deuce was only vaguely aware of their route. His attention was riveted on Grace. They said little as they walked but fell into a comfortable pace. She seemed to trust him completely and the few times he steered her around passersby, she responded as if they had been walking together for years.

Finally, she said, "This is the corridor. It's the third door on the left."

"Third on the left," Deuce repeated. He counted the doors until they reached hers.

She turned toward him, her face turned up toward his. Although her eyes were unfocused, he had the unnerving sensation that she was looking at him.

"How do you do that?" he asked again.

She smiled. "I cheat," she whispered with a conspiratorial wink. "The pendant is a piezoelectric crystal. It sends out ultrasonic impulses. I have receivers implanted in my skull that pick up the return vibrations and translate them into a sound picture. I can 'see' in sonar, not details, but enough to pick out rough shapes. I really am blind like a bat."

Deuce laughed. "You didn't really need me, did you?"

"A lady always has use for a strong arm to hold," she said.

"How touching," said a voice from Deuce's right.

He turned, cursing himself for being careless. A lean black man in a well-cut gray business suit leaned against the wall, a meter or so away. Deuce hadn't heard him approach but he did hear the scrape of a boot from behind. He turned slowly and saw two more men coming up the corridor. These two wore utilitarian jump suits and, although they carried no weapons, they had the unmistakable look of hired muscle.

Deuce turned back to the man in the business suit. "What do you want?"

The man ignored him. "You've been avoiding me, Grace," he said. "That's not smart."

"I told you I was finished, Lucas," Grace said evenly. "I don't owe Jones anything anymore."

"It doesn't work that way, Grace," said Lucas. "We paid for your fancy implants for a reason. You work for us until we say the job is finished."

"The lady said she quit," Deuce said quietly. "Why don't you just walk away?"

"This is none of your business, big man." Lucas held out his left hand, palm up so Deuce could see it clearly. Tattooed there was a green and white shield with a rearing red dragon in its center, the sign of the Red Dragons.

"It'll take more'n a pretty tattoo to make me run away with my tail between my legs." Deuce eased Grace's hand off his arm and placed her gently against the door. "You sure you want to make this play?"

Lucas moved away from the wall and faced Deuce. He flicked his arm downward and a short-bladed combat knife dropped from a wrist sheath into his hand. Deuce crouched, aware of the footsteps of the men moving up behind him. He watched Lucas's eyes. They flicked up and to the left and Deuce sensed movement behind him. He lashed out with his left leg and caught the man behind him in the knee. The joint gave way with a distinct pop and the thug went down screaming.

Deuce feinted toward the other thug and Lucas grinned, rushing forward with the knife. But Deuce swung his body to meet him as he drove forward with his right leg. He brought both fists up, smashed into Lucas's chest and continued to drive forward. The combined force of Deuce's blow and Lucas's own momentum cracked the black man's sternum and momentarily took his breath away. Deuce didn't let up but kept driving into him, pummeling fists into his gut and ribs. The knife raked across Deuce's left arm drawing blood but doing little damage.

Lucas stumbled back, stunned, then lost his footing and fell backwards, arms flailing. Deuce caught his right hand and twisted. The knife clattered to the floor as bones snapped in Lucas's wrist. Deuce swept up the knife with one hand and smashed the heel of the other into Lucas's nose.

The third man rushed Deuce from behind, wrapping a thick forearm around his neck. Before the thug could lock his arm into a knockout hold, Deuce slashed his elbow with the knife. The man's grip loosened and Deuce tucked his chin and turned his head. He elbowed the thug in the gut and he let go. Deuce grabbed the man by his injured elbow and swung him head first into the wall.

Deuce held the knife in a low fighting grip as he backed up to cover Grace. She palmed the lock to her apartment and the door swung open. Lucas struggled to his feet, breathing in short, wheezing gasps. The two other men stayed down, not wanting to engage Deuce again.

"Told you you didn't want to make that play," Deuce said. "Enough?"

Lucas nodded. "You're not helping her, you know."

"Maybe not. But I won't be leaving her."

Lucas shrugged. "Your call, soldier. We'll be back."

"I'm counting on it." Deuce felt Grace's hand on the back of his shirt pulling him into the apartment. He watched as Lucas struggled to straighten up and walk away, then he backed in through the door and closed it.

He turned to face Grace and she fell against his chest, wrapping her arms around him. He hesitated for a second, and then held her close. His arm began to throb where the knife had sliced him.

"Oh, Sven," she said, her voice muffled by his broad chest. "I was so frightened."

That made him laugh. "If you're gonna snuggle me like that, I'll forget you set me up. But don't lie to me. You ain't been scared of anything for years."

She started to push him away, but he gripped her upper arms. She struggled for a second, then stopped and stood very still. "What are you going to do?" she asked.

"I'm going to let go of your arms and then you're going to tell me what the Dragons want with you." She nodded once and he opened his hands. She stepped back, but not very far. She reached out and touched his left arm. Her fingers came away sticky with blood.

"You're hurt," she said.

"Just a scratch."

"I'll get you a clean towel. I don't have an autodoc in the apartment, or even bandages."

"Clean cloth's all it needs," said Deuce. He followed her into a small utility room and she pulled out a white face towel. Deuce wrapped his arm with it, wincing as he cinched it tight across the shallow slash in his biceps. *It could use a stitch or two,* he thought. But a trip to a clinic would lead to too many questions.

Grace stood with her back to the wall. Deuce took her by the arm and guided her back to the apartment's main room. It was comfortably if functionally furnished with a pair of overstuffed armchairs, a low table and a small sofa. She sat down in one of the armchairs and pulled her knees up to her chin. Deuce lowered himself onto the sofa, facing her.

"So, why me?" asked Deuce. "Was it just my lucky day?"

She frowned. "You make it sound colder than it was. I knew Lucas would be waiting and Henry isn't very intimidating. I didn't think he'd actually confront us. I thought he'd see I had an escort and wait until later."

"How much later? Was I supposed to be your bodyguard all night?

"It wasn't like that, Sven. I just needed a strong arm to get me home."

"Lucas is a soldier for the Dragons. He's not gonna leave you alone just because I walk you home. What'd you think would happen tomorrow? Or the next day?"

"One day is all I need," she said.

"How's that?"

She sighed. "I had a plan. If I can get to the spaceport by ten in the morning, I can catch a ride on a Kwai Hong freighter bound for Delilah. Li set it up. I paid the pilot three thousand yuan to get me off Ceres."

"You trust this pilot?"

"I trust Li. He may not be the businessman his father is, but he's sweet and has always been honest with me."

"Lucas said the Dragons paid for your implants. What's the deal there?" Grace didn't answer. Deuce continued, "Is it a killing matter, or do they just want to rough you up a bit?"

She frowned. "Given a choice, I'd still rather not be beaten up."

"Not what I meant. So far, all I've done is play rough with Lucas and the boys. Now they know they can't push me around. The Dragons can call it a misunderstanding and save face." Deuce paused for a second. "But if I draw first blood and they don't mean to kill you, then I could turn this into something it ain't. I need to know what the stakes are."

Grace nodded. "I was a tunnel singer in Planetia when they found me. I sang for tips near the Po Han Square drop shafts."

Deuce nodded. "I know the place. Tough crowd."

"It wasn't so bad. I managed to stay alive and avoided the worst of the gangs for a while. Then Lucas approached me and asked me how I'd like a steady gig singing in a night club. I didn't buy it at first, but he offered me twenty yuan to meet with another man at a public cafe. The other man never told me his name, but I think it was Colin Jones."

"Jones offered you the job?"

Grace nodded. "They paid for the implants so I could find my way around without help. They got me the job singing at the club here on Ceres. I was supposed to get close to Kwai Li Fan and then use him to access company secrets. But Li isn't the old man's choice to run things here. The real power has been given to the number two son, Kwai Chang Wu."

"So now the Dragons want you to seduce Wu?" Deuce asked.

Grace shivered and nodded. "I didn't mind making a play for Li Fan. He's not a bad guy and he treats the employees at the club all right. But Wu scares me. I met him once when he came to the club to talk to Li. He's cold; like an AI, no spark of warmth in his voice. He shook my hand, and I felt like I'd touched a corpse."

"You told Lucas you wouldn't do it," Deuce said flatly.

"Not right then. I tried to be friendly to Wu, if not seductive. He was polite enough but made it clear he wasn't interested. As near as I can tell from what Li says, his brother lives like a monk. He sleeps on the floor in his office, eats little, never drinks and never, never fraternizes with the help. I told Lucas there wasn't a chance he'd let me get anything on him, but the Dragons aren't letting me off the hook. Lucas insists there's got to be some way to get to Wu and that I have to find it."

Deuce nodded. "I can't see them wanting you dead over this. It'd be too much trouble to cover their tracks, even if they brought in outside talent. Lucas's not hiding his tattoo and those goons he was with were locals. They were sending you a message: play ball or else."

"What do we do now?" asked Grace.

"We?"

She touched his arm and he laughed.

"Okay, we. First we need something more than this knife before we meet up with any of Lucas's friends. Don't suppose you've got a pulse rifle stashed around here?" She shook her head. "No, didn't think so," he said. "How about a public netlink?"

"Why not the one in the apartment?" she asked.

"If they're not tapped into it, they're stupid. And they ain't stupid."

"There's a public link two corridors over near the store."

Deuce rose. "I need to get in touch with my brother. Stay here, lock the door behind me. Don't open it for anyone but me."

A few minutes later Deuce stood in front of a small public holomatrix. Mike answered as soon as Deuce gave his password.

"Deuce, what's wrong?" Mike asked. "Why aren't you using your personal link?"

"Spot of trouble," Deuce said. "I need you to get the brown leather bag I use for my surveying gear and bring it to this address." He read the address from the storefront. "Leg it, bro. This one has a sell-by date."

"On my way," Mike answered. "Give me twenty minutes."

Sixteen minutes later, Deuce saw Mike approaching from a cross passageway. He lifted a hand in greeting and Mike quickened his pace.

"So what's the play, big brother?" Mike asked. "Are we going to war?" Deuce cocked his head and Mike grinned. "Yeah, I know what you have in the bag. I always thought it looked too heavy for survey equipment."

"Follow me." Deuce took the bag from Mike.

They made their way back to Grace's apartment. Deuce knocked twice, then twice again. Grace answered through the door, her voice muffled.

"Is that you, Sven?"

Mike grinned and whispered, "Sven?"

"Shut up," Deuce whispered back before answering Grace in a loud voice, "Yes, it's me. My brother's with me. You can open the door."

The door seals hissed and the door popped inward. Deuce stepped in. Grace had moved away from the door to the other side of the sofa. Deuce nodded his approval, even though she couldn't see the gesture. She was cautious and that was good. He waved Mike inside and resealed the door.

"It's okay, Grace," Deuce said stepping up to take her hand. She held it tight, then faced Mike.

"You're Sven's brother?"

Mike offered his hand before realizing she couldn't see it. "I'm Mike Finney," he said reaching out to touch her fingertips.

She shook his hand. "Finney? Not Gulbrandsen?"

"My Ma was a widow for a few years before she married Mike's Dad," said Deuce. "I was grown and on my own by then. Mike and I teamed up after he finished school."

"Deuce needed a keeper, so I promised Mom I'd look out for him," Mike said.

Deuce grunted and Grace laughed. "I see. So, Sven is watching out for me and you're watching out for him."

Deuce ignored the banter and flipped the bag upside down on the low table. He touched releases on diagonally opposite corners and lifted the false bottom away from the rest of the bag. Nestled in the shallow compartment under it lay a pulse rifle, broken down into power chamber, barrel and stock, along with a pair of combat knives and a blackened steel Smith and Wesson needler. A separate compartment held two power packs for the rifle and several spare magazines for the Smith and Wesson.

Deuce rapidly assembled the pulse rifle and clipped a power pack into the stock. Mike picked up the needler and a mag. Grace ran her hands over the pulse rifle, the knives and the needler, then drew back.

"Who are you?" she asked.

Mike laughed as he clicked the magazine into place. "I thought you already knew," he said. "Deuce is First Sergeant Sven Gulbrandsen, Martian Third Directorate."

Grace gasped. "The death squads."

"No!" Deuce growled. "Those were the Black Ops crew. I was counterinsurgency."

Mike touched Grace on the shoulder. "He's one of the good guys, Grace," he said softly. Then louder to Deuce, "So what's the plan, big brother?"

"We stay with Grace tonight, get her to the spaceport tomorrow."

"Something tells me it isn't that simple. Otherwise, you wouldn't need me or the bag."

"Just before I called you, I roughed up a soldier for the Red Dragons who tried to muscle Grace. They may try to stop us."

Mike whistled softly. "Do you look for trouble, bro? Or does it just find you?"

Deuce shrugged. "I warned them. I ain't gonna let a cheap *baotu* with a fancy tattoo scare me off."

"Is this about Grace, or about you?"

"I told Grace I'd protect her."

Mike sighed. "Okay, Deuce. What's at the spaceport?"

Grace spoke up. "I paid a freighter pilot to get me off Ceres. The freighter's leaving for Delilah tomorrow morning. From there I can catch a transport to Tharsis or Tycho."

"And the Dragons?"

75

Deuce hefted the pulse rifle. "We can deal with them."

"Think, big brother," Mike said. "What happens when the freighter gets to Delilah? And even if they don't get Grace there, what about Tharsis? That's Dragon country. They'll snatch her as soon as the transport docks. Tycho isn't much better. Are you going to stay with her forever?"

"You got a better idea?"

Mike turned to Grace. "Why are the Dragons after you?"

Grace hesitated for a second, but Deuce nudged her gently. "It's Okay. Mikey's the smart one. He can help."

Grace nodded and told Mike about the implants and her contract at the club. "I was supposed to get close to Li and use him to report back to Lucas on Kwai Hong business secrets. But old man Kwai doesn't have any confidence in Li Fan. He may be the oldest son, but he doesn't have any real power in the family business."

Mike nodded. "That's true. The word in the business media is that Li is a half-wit and Kwai Hong has disowned him. Kwai Chang Wu is supposed to be taking over all the operations here on Ceres. That's really unusual for someone like Kwai Hong, who touts himself as a Chinese traditionalist."

"Li's not stupid," Grace said. "He's just disinterested. He'd rather run a nightclub than a billion yuan conglomerate. I've met Wu. He's a cold as ice. Everyone here is afraid of him."

"So the Dragons want you to shift your attentions to Wu?"

Grace nodded. "Except, Wu's not interested. I tried to tell Lucas that it's a dead end, but he won't listen."

"What sort of information were you supposed to be gathering?" asked Mike.

"I don't know. Lucas just said he'd tell me when the time came."

Mike pursed his lips. "Why would the Dragons go to so much trouble to spy on Kwai Hong?"

"Don't matter what they want," growled Deuce. "Grace ain't working for them anymore and they don't like it."

Mike nodded thoughtfully. "That's the immediate

situation, bro. Just wondering how important Grace is to them and why." He looked at Grace but didn't ask her any more questions. "So what's our next move? Stay here or get to the spaceport before the Dragons can arrange a reception?"

"Best we move Grace to our room," Deuce said. "The Dragons'll be watching the Port. Lucas won't take a chance on her getting away without a fight. It'll take them a while to figure out who I am, and that gives us a window to get out of here." He touched Grace on the shoulder and she leaned into him wearily. "Get what you need to take with you and we'll leave right away."

She nodded. She made her way to the small bedroom and returned almost immediately with a shoulder bag slung over her arm. "I'm ready. I've had this packed since I first talked to Li about getting out of here."

Mike looked thoughtful again, but Deuce didn't care. He had a mission and a plan and that was all he needed.

"Stay here while I check the corridor," he said. "Mikey, keep the door open a crack so you can see me. Bring Grace along when I signal you."

Mike stood in the doorway as Deuce edged down the corridor. He reached the junction and checked the main passageway as far as the drop shafts. Then he waved Mike forward. As soon as he heard Mike and Grace come up behind him, he started off down the main passageway. He held the pulse rifle at low ready and hoped he wouldn't have to use it.

The walk back to the guest quarters where Deuce and Mike shared a room took only a few minutes. It was late in the sleep cycle and most of the workers in the area were home in bed. Deuce covered the corridor as Mike opened the door and ushered Grace in. Deuce scanned the area but saw no one. Still, he had a feeling the Dragons knew exactly where they were.

Deuce put Grace in his bed and spent the night on the floor in front of the door. Mike sat up in a chair for a long time, eyes closed but still awake. Deuce woke up several times during the night and saw him sitting in the same place, but by the time Grace awoke, Mike had moved to the other bed.

Deuce sat up as soon as Grace stirred and was standing by the door when she sat up in bed. "Sleep well?" he asked.

"Fine," she said. A note of concern crept into her voice. "Did you sit up all night?"

"No, I cat napped here by the door. An old military trick. I'm fine." He didn't mention that Mike had been awake most of the night.

"What time is it?" she asked.

"Six-thirty local," said Deuce. "What time are you supposed to meet this freighter pilot?"

"Eight. The ship is supposed to leave at ten-forty."

"Right. Shake Mikey and wake him up. We leave in ten. I'm going to scout the front."

He lifted his jacket from a hook near the door and draped it over the pulse rifle. No sense in scaring the civilians. A quick check of the lobby and the front of the guest quarters revealed nothing more threatening than a pair of data technicians sipping coffee on a bench near the entrance to the tube station.

He returned to the room to find Grace dressed in traveling clothes—slacks and a light jacket. Mike was up and had packed Deuce's kit in a shoulder bag.

"I put your share of our fee in there, too," Mike said softly. "Fifty-five hundred yuan. You may need it."

"What about you, bro?" Deuce asked. "Not packed?"

"No," said Mike. "I'm staying on Ceres. You go with Grace, I'll catch up to you on Delilah."

Deuce frowned. "Why?"

"There's a reason Jones wants to spy on the Kwai's and it's here on Ceres. I'll help you get Grace to the spaceport, then see what I can find out here."

Deuce shook his head. "Don't like that much. Too risky."

"Remember what I said last night. You can't protect Grace forever. If I know what Jones wants, maybe I can persuade him she's not a threat."

"I understand that. Still don't mean I like it."

Mike shrugged but didn't say anything more.

Deuce took the lead, placing Grace behind him with Mike in the rear. He kept the pulse rifle, still draped in the jacket, at low ready. Mike had his hand in his jacket pocket, gripping the needler. They crossed the wide junction of passageways that fronted the guest quarters and headed toward the tube station. The Dragons jumped them as they passed the last corridor before the station entrance.

Lucas stepped out from the side corridor flanked by two more big men in dark suits. All three of them held short-barreled pneumatics. Lucas sported a transparent splint on his wrist but otherwise looked none the worse for wear. Deuce swung toward him, leveling the pulse rifle. Mike grunted a warning as two more Dragons stepped out of the tube station.

"I told you we'd be back," said Lucas. "You can still walk away, if Grace comes with us. This isn't your fight, soldier."

Deuce thumbed the safety off the pulse rifle. "Not gonna happen," he said.

Lucas smiled slightly as he raised the pneumatic. The smile froze on his face as a bolt from the pulse rifle burned through his chest. Deuce was already leaping to one side as Lucas began to fall. The pulse rifle sizzled again and the Dragon to Lucas's right went down. From behind him, Deuce could hear the distinct *snap-ping* sound of a needler. The remaining Dragon in front of him fell as Mike's needle stuck in his neck.

Deuce rolled to his back as his shoulder hit the deck and swung the pulse rifle to cover the Dragons from the tube station. Pneumatic rounds spalled off the deck next to him. Mike cried out and fell, clutching his thigh. The needler clattered on the deck. Deuce fired twice and dropped one of the Dragons. The second man ducked behind a support pillar and the bolt of coherent energy cracked and sparked as it dissipated through the pillar.

Deuce rolled to his left and came up onto his knees, swinging the pulse rifle to cover the pillar. He saw the barrel of the pneumatic, wide as a tunnel, pointing straight at his head and knew he was an instant too slow.

He heard the sound of a needler and the pneumatic wavered, then dropped to the deck as the Dragon holding it crumpled. Deuce rose to his feet and lowered the pulse rifle.

"Easy, Grace," he said. "You got him. I'm to your right and I'm gonna take that needler. Okay?"

She nodded but held the needler in a two handed grip, still pointing it at the Dragon on the deck. Two needles protruded from the man's neck. Deuce reached out and closed his hand gently on the needler. She released it and stepped into his arms.

"Mikey, you okay?" Deuce asked.

"I'm alive. Hurts like hell, though."

Deuce released Grace and knelt next to Mike, who sat on the deck with a bloody hand clutching the wound in his leg. Deuce gently examined the wound and flexed Mike's knee and hip.

"Clean wound," he said. "Through and through. Missed the bone. Can you move it?"

"Yeah," Mike said, hissing as Deuce hauled him to his feet. "Not going to get very far, though."

"Just need to get to the tube station. I can carry you that far."

Mike pulled away, wincing as he limped on his injured leg. "Get Grace to the spaceport. Take her to Delilah. Watch over her. I'll meet you on Delilah in a week or so."

"Mike, don't be stupid. We gotta be someplace else when the cops show up."

Mike shook his head. "If somebody isn't here when the cops show up, that freighter will never leave the dock. There are five dead Dragons here."

"Only three," Deuce said. "The needler's loaded with sleepers."

"All the more reason I need to stay. You want them to be the only ones the cops talk to?"

"This ain't your fight, Mike. I shouldn't have dragged you into it, but I ain't leaving you behind."

Mike grabbed him by the shoulder. "You're not. This is a tactical retreat. Think of me as the rear guard." He winced again and laughed.

Deuce frowned. "No jokes, Mike."

"Not joking, big brother. Take Grace and go. I'll have your back. It'll be okay."

Deuce held his eye for a moment, then drew him close. "Ma told me to look out for you."

"And you have," said Mike. "I'll keep the cops busy until you're on your way."

Deuce nodded and slung the pulse rifle over his shoulder. He took Grace by the arm and steered her into the tube station. After another backward glance at Mike, he entered the code for the spaceport and a capsule detached itself from the stream and hissed to a stop in front of them. Deuce popped open the hatch and helped Grace into the front seat. He stowed the pulse rifle behind the second seat and climbed in next to her. The hatch swung closed and the capsule sped off into the tube. Grace clung to his arm. Deuce stared into the blank darkness as the capsule sped along.

"Will he be alright?" Grace asked. "Mike, I mean."

"Hope so."

"Was he right? The needler was loaded with sleeper darts?"

"Yeah."

"Then the man I shot isn't..."

"Dead?" said Deuce. He put his arm around her. "No. He'll wake up in a few hours with a hell of a headache, that's all."

Grace laid her head on his shoulder. "Good."

"Good shooting for a bind girl, though," Deuce said. Grace smiled and looked up at him. He lifted her chin with the thumb and forefinger of his free hand and kissed her upturned lips. She kissed him back and he held her close for several heartbeats. "Well, alright then," he said when he could breathe again.

The capsule chimed before Grace could answer and slowed to a stop at the spaceport. The hatch hissed open and Deuce jumped out. He retrieved his pulse rifle before helping Grace out.

"What freighter are we looking for?"

"The *Tokai Maru*, dock 34," she said. "What time is it?"

"Quarter to eight. Plenty of time."

Grace nodded, holding tightly to his arm. Deuce scanned the glowing status display hanging above the concourse and found the right dock. The spaceport was empty save a few crewmen milling about the transients lounge. Ceres was an industrial port. No one visited casually. Most loading and off-loading was automated and freighter crews tended to stay aboard ship for a quick departure once their loadout was finished.

They found dock 34 at the far end of the main concourse. Deuce thumbed the intercom button next to the airlock. After a few seconds a tinny voice answered.

"Yeah? Who the hell are you?"

Deuce looked into the video pickup. "Name's Gulbrandsen. I brought your fare." He moved so that the pickup focused on Grace.

"You're early," the man on the intercom said.

"I didn't want to miss the boat." Grace said. "Li made it clear you wouldn't wait for me."

"You got the cash?" Grace nodded. "Then kiss your boyfriend good-bye and come on aboard."

"Change of plans. I'm coming, too," said Deuce.

"Not the deal, friend. One passenger only."

"Two or not at all. I'll pay."

The man on the intercom didn't answer right away. Then he said, "Ten thousand."

"Three," said Deuce. "Plus the three she's already paid you."

"Three thousand was the security deposit. She still owes me two. Ten thousand for the two of you."

"I got fifty-five hundred cash on me," Deuce said. "That's eighty-five hundred all together. Take it or I make a call to customs about the contraband you've got in your lifeboats." The threat was a wild guess, Deuce knew, but smuggling was a way of life for Belt pilots, and he figured the odds were on his side.

"You're bluffing."

"Okay, let's make a call and find out." Deuce kept his voice flat and matter of fact.

"Alright," the man growled. "Eighty-five. And you

82

better have the cash."

The airlock hissed and opened. Deuce cradled the pulse rifle under his arm and guided Grace through the lock. The inner hatch opened into the control room of the freighter's travel head. To their right was a command chair and a control panel facing a large view screen. To the left, a hatch led to the rest of the ship.

"Lose the hardware and show me some money," said a voice from their left.

Deuce looked toward the voice and saw a tall figure half concealed behind the hatch coaming. The man's face was in shadow, but the arm holding the pneumatic was clearly visible. Deuce carefully lowered the pulse rifle to the floor and held out his hands, palms open.

"Easy, friend," he said. "I'm gonna get the cash out of my kit."

The tall man stepped out from the hatch, still holding the pneumatic leveled at Deuce's head. He wore a one-piece jumpsuit with a Ceres Mining and Manufacturing logo on the left chest area. His shaved scalp gleamed in the light of the control room and a sparse red beard covered his chin. His hand shook slightly as he stepped forward and nudged the pulse rifle out of Deuce's reach with his foot.

Deuce pulled a bundle of notes from his kit bag and showed it to the pilot. The tall man eyed him cautiously, then motioned with his free hand. Deuce leaned toward him and held out the cash. As the pilot's finger touched the bundle, Deuce let it drop. The tall man made a grab for the cash and Deuce surged forward, driving his forearm into the pilot's throat. He grabbed the pneumatic with his other hand and wrenched it free. The pilot fell to his knees coughing and clutching at his neck.

"Jesus, man," coughed the pilot. "You like to killed me."

Deuce held the pneumatic pointed at the floor. "We had a deal. I don't like having guns pointed at me."

"A man's gotta protect himself." The tall man took a deep wheezing breath and picked up the bundle of cash. He struggled to his feet. "You're the one who came in here packing hardware."

Deuce smiled. "A man's gotta protect himself." He reversed the pneumatic and offered it butt first. "We good?"

The pilot took the weapon and tucked it into his belt. Then he fanned the cash in his hand and did a quick count. He nodded. "We're good. You're Gulbrandsen? I'm Tucker. Pick up your gear and follow me."

Tucker led them down a narrow passageway to a cluster of tiny compartments that opened off of a common dining area. He pointed to the right.

"That one's yours. I'm in the middle. That one is Sato's. He's the engineer; sleeps with his precious engines most of the time. You won't see much of him but don't mess with his cabin. He's real twitchy about people messing with his stuff."

Deuce led Grace to the small cabin. A single bunk was attached to the bulkhead on the left. A water dispenser, small sink and toilet unit and a battered metal and plastic chair completed the furnishings. Grace sat on the bunk as Deuce stowed his kit and the pulse rifle under it. He stood in the center of the cabin and stretched his arms. His fingertips brushed the bulkheads on either side.

"Are you okay?" he asked, looking down at her. She nodded, still clutching her small travel bag. "You want me to stow that for you?"

She shook her head and began groping in the bag she held. Her movements became more frantic as tears flooded her eyes and ran down her cheeks. Finally she found what she was looking for and pulled out a handful of hundred yuan notes.

"I'll pay you the rest when I can," she said, pushing the cash toward him.

"You don't owe me anything," Deuce said.

"But you gave Tucker all the money you earned. I can't let you do that."

Deuce sat on the bunk next to her and covered her hands with his. "Yes, you can. I want to do this, Grace. I'd just blow it on something stupid anyway."

She continued to push the money into his hands for

a second then gave up. He took the cash from her and tucked it back into her bag. He closed the bag and put it next to his kit on the deck under the bunk. He started to stand, but her hands found his again and she held them tightly.

"Don't leave me, Deuce. I don't think I can do this alone."

He pulled her close and kissed her. The kiss lasted a long time. Then Deuce reached out, closed the hatch and turned off the light. They hardly noticed when the travel head disengaged from the dock and boosted up to the orbiting engineering module and cargo spine that comprised most of the bulk of the *Tokai Maru*.

A few hours after the ship left Ceres' orbit, Deuce emerged from the cabin and surveyed the small common area of the living quarters. Tucker looked up from a bowl of noodles with a sly smile but had the good sense to keep silent after a glare from Deuce.

"Food dispenser's on the starboard bulkhead," was all he said as he slurped noodles.

Deuce nodded his thanks and dialed up a couple of ramen bowels. He returned to the small cabin with the steaming food and closed the door again.

Delilah was antegrade relative to Ceres and the downhill run only took three days, even for a large freighter like the *Tokai*. Deuce and Grace spent much of the voyage in the tiny cabin, oblivious to the passage of time.

"What about Customs?" Deuce asked as Tucker guided the travel head into Delilah's huge cargo dock. He and Grace stood behind the command chair where Tucker sat.

"This is Delilah, man. Nobody cares who comes and goes. Customs won't look past my manifest." He engaged the landing skids and settled the craft to the deck. The dock pressurized with a hiss of fog and vapor and the gravity generators spun up to one G.

Tucker turned his head to look at Grace. "Welcome to Delilah, the ass end of the solar system." Grace just smiled and Tucker shrugged.

Deuce looked out through the forward view screen.

"Company," he said. The personnel lock hissed open and a small thin man stepped into the dock. "I thought you said Customs wouldn't care who came and went."

Tucker looked closely at the man crossing the dock toward them. "Shit," he whispered. "That ain't Customs. He's Patel, an enforcer for the Dragons." He looked at Grace again. "Who did you piss off, lady?"

Deuce kept his eye on the approaching figure as he dropped his kit to the deck and swung the pulse rifle down from his shoulder. "Stay here, Grace. Tucker, can you close the forward hatch from here?"

"Sure."

"Then as soon as I clear the outer hatch, close it and seal it tight."

"No, Sven," Grace said. "Stay here. He can't get in without help. He can't, right Tucker?"

"Not without a laser torch. 'Course, we can't get out past him either."

Deuce touched Grace on the arm. "And that's why you're going to seal that hatch after me. If he's alone, I can take him. If he's got help, you and Tucker can hole up here until Mike can get you out."

He flicked the pulse rifle's safety off and the reaction chamber whined as it charged up. He walked over to the forward hatch and opened it. "Seal the outer door as soon as I'm outside," he told Tucker.

Deuce stepped into the lock and closed the hatch. He brought the pulse rifle up to his shoulder and opened the outer hatch. He stepped through and swept the rifle right to cover the man standing in the open dock. The hatch hissed closed behind him. The other man didn't move.

"I'd appreciate it if you'd point that rifle elsewhere, soldier," he said.

Deuce kept the weapon leveled at him. "Who are you and what do you want?"

"My name's Ashok Patel. I have a message for Grace Tyler from my boss, Colin Jones. I think you know who he is."

"I know. Give me the message; I'll pass it along to Grace."

Patel smiled. "Made herself another friend, did she? Okay, soldier, we'll do it your way." His voice hardened. "As soon as you lower that pulse rifle, we'll give you a pass on killing Lucas. I never liked the little bastard, anyway. But this deal is only good right here, right now."

Deuce hesitated, then moved the pulse rifle to low ready. "What've you got to say?"

"Tell your new girlfriend she's on her own from now on. As long as she stays away from our business interests, she's free to ply her trade wherever she likes."

Deuce twitched the rifle up. "Watch your tone. She ain't a whore."

Patel smiled thinly. "Whatever you say, soldier. That's the deal. Tell her if she shows her pretty face on Ceres again, she's dead." He turned his back and walked away as if Deuce wasn't there.

"Does it work both ways?" Deuce called after him.

Patel stopped and looked over his shoulder. "How's that?"

"If I see you or any of your boys near Grace, do I get to shoot you?"

"Don't push your luck, soldier."

Deuce sighted along the barrel of the pulse rifle. "Ain't never been lucky. But I am a damn good shot."

Patel eyed him coolly. "I'll remember that." He turned again and walked out of the dock.

Deuce lowered the pulse rifle and rubbed his scalp. The hatched hissed open behind him. Tucker and Grace stood in the lock.

"I told you to wait inside," said Deuce.

"I told Tucker to bring me out," answered Grace. "I'm through with hiding."

"No need now; as long as you stay away from the Dragons, they'll give you a pass. Must be something big going on back on Ceres, or they wouldn't be so hot to keep you away from the Kwai's."

Grace shivered. "I don't ever plan to go back there again."

Deuce smiled. "Good." He took her hand and slung the pulse rifle. "You know a decent place to rent a room here, Tucker?"

He grinned. "My cousin has a nice place. Only twenty yuan a night, meals included."

Deuce laughed. "For twenty yuan, your cousin better be a damn good cook."

"She is," Tucker nodded eagerly. "Come on. Her place is just three decks down and a little west of here."

Tucker's cousin proved to be a very good cook, indeed. The room was spacious by Belt standards, clean and simply furnished. Deuce sent a message to Mike over the public net and they settled down to wait for a reply.

Mike arrived three days later to find Deuce and Grace sharing breakfast. He noticed the change in them as he sat down at the table and poured some coffee from the carafe in the center.

"You two look like an old married couple," he said, sipping the hot liquid.

Grace smiled and Deuce leaned back in his chair rubbing his scalp. "Well, now. Hadn't really thought much on that," he said.

Mike laughed. "Just saying, that's all. I guess you got the word that Grace is free to go as far as the Dragons are concerned."

Deuce nodded. "A guy named Patel, enforcer type with a real high opinion of himself, met us at the dock. Said Grace was off the hook but oughta stay away from Ceres if she wanted to keep breathing."

Mike nodded. "She'd be advised to avoid Tharsis as well. Jones seemed keen to keep her away from anywhere they had 'business interests,' as he put it."

Deuce shrugged. "No problem. There's lots of clubs in the Belt or on the Moon she can sing at."

Grace shifted uneasily and Mike said softly, "But that creates a problem for Grace doesn't it?"

"Say what?"

Mike took her hand. She made as if to pull it away but stopped. "When were you going to tell him?" Mike asked. "Jones had it figured out. That's why he sent Lucas after you. Once I convinced him that exposing you solved his problem, he agreed that killing you was bad business, no matter how the war played out."

"Tell me what," demanded Deuce. "Grace, what's he talking about?"

"Grace hasn't played straight with you, big brother. Those fancy implants of hers are a little too high end even for a rich gangster like Jones. They're military grade technology."

"Sven, I meant to tell you once the *Tokai* left orbit," Grace interrupted. "But then you were willing to give up everything just to keep me safe and we kissed and it all got complicated." She wiped a tear from her eye and sat straight in the chair, her face suddenly hard. "I'm Martian, first, last and always. It wasn't the Dragons who found me in that dropshaft plaza in Planetia. It was the Third Directorate. I was on Ceres working for Martian Intelligence."

"Metternich," spat Deuce. "You're working for Metternich."

"I tried to let you know in the club, when we first talked, when we drank that toast. You used to work for them, too."

"Nothing like a termination order to cure a person of that."

"I was supposed to work inside the Dragons' organization," Grace said in a rush, as if Deuce would get up and leave before she could finish. "They've always been strong in Tharsis, even during the war, and we still don't know where their base in the Belt is hidden. I was supposed to find out."

"Why? So Metternich could take it out and break up their operations in Tharsis?" asked Deuce. "I ain't never been partial to them, but if the Dragons are making things hard for Colonel Metternich, then more power to them."

"I'm sorry I didn't tell you, Sven. And for what it's worth, when I paid Tucker to get me out of Ceres, it wasn't Lucas I was afraid of. I knew by then that I couldn't go through with the mission. The things I learned about how the Death Squads were purging Tharsis and Planetia were unbelievable at first. But the Dragons have sources in both places and the truth is getting out through them."

Deuce exhaled loudly. "Well, you played me to the end. I'll get my kit, and Mike and I will shove off. " He stood. "Have a nice life, Grace."

She reached out and grabbed his hand. "No, Sven, wait," she pleaded. "I know I wasn't honest with you, but what we had on the *Tokai*, and here on Delilah, that's all real. I didn't mean to have feelings for you. I tried not to. I tried to just play the part and keep you close for protection. But you were willing to give up everything you'd earned to stay with me. You never pushed or pressured me. How could I not love that?" Deuce didn't move and she pulled his hand to her lips and kissed it. "Please, Sven. Let me start over."

"It takes more than a few nights of hot sex to make this alright, Grace." Deuce's voice was soft and quavered as he spoke. "How can I trust anything you say?"

"Seems to me, the lady's asking for a chance to earn that," Mike said. "For what it's worth, brother, Jones intercepted a copy of the letter of resignation she sent to Mars just before you met up with her at that bar."

"*Honto?*" Deuce looked down at Grace.

"Yes."

"Metternich will be out for your blood, too," he said, taking her hand in both of his.

She nodded. "You think you're the only enemy of the state out here in the Belt?"

He pulled her to her feet and took her into his arms. "Don't you ever lie to me again."

"Never, Sven." She turned her face up to his and he kissed her, long and slow.

"Well, then," said Mike. "I guess I'll just leave you two alone. And since it sounds like you blew all your cash again, I guess I'll have to spring for our passage home."

Deuce lifted his head long enough to say, "I'll pay you back, bro."

"Sure you will." Mike turned and left them there, locked in each other's arms.

* * *

Deuce shook his head as he came back to the present. They still sat on the floor of the nightclub on Highpoint. Grace nestled under his arm. He felt a surge of regret for what might have been.

"We could have had a good life together," sighed Grace, echoing his feelings.

"I thought we were building that."

She sat up straighter. "But you never said anything. You never asked."

"No, I didn't. Didn't think I had to," Deuce said. "I'm asking now, Grace."

"What?" she gasped. She pulled away, but he held her.

"Hear me out, Grace. I didn't know what I wanted until now. Wouldn't have worked anyhow, not with the way I been living. But things are different. We, Zack and me, we got steady work. A real business. You and I could make a go of it, now."

"No, Sven, we couldn't. It's too late for us."

Deuce gripped her arms. "No it isn't. You've got to believe that. I won't let you go again." His link chimed, but he ignored it as he searched Grace's face for some hint of agreement.

"Deuce, this is a priority override," Sylvia's voice said in his ear. "Zack wants you back on the *Profit* right away. We have a job."

"Then Zack can call me himself and not get his AI to do it."

"That was uncalled for Deuce." Sylvia's voice was cold and hurt at the same time. "I may be the ship's AI, but I have feelings too."

"What is it, Sven?" asked Grace.

"Call from my ship's AI. We have a job. Zack wants me back aboard ASAP."

"So go. I'm not going anywhere. Not for six weeks anyway. That's how much I have left on this contract."

"I'm not leaving until you tell me you'll think about what I said."

Grace sighed. "Yes, Sven. I'll think about it. If you come back..."

"I'll be back," Deuce interrupted.

"If you come back, we'll talk," she said.

Deuce pulled her close and kissed her. She touched his cheek as he started to turn away.

"I want to believe, Sven," she whispered. "Come back to me."

He nodded and climbed to his feet. "On my way, Sylvia," he said into his link. He lifted Grace to her feet, touched her lips gently and then turned and walked out of the club.

Grace watched him until he disappeared through the door. The tears she had held back began to flow down her cheeks and a single sob escaped her.

"Touching," said a male voice from behind her.

"Shut up," she said without turning around.

"When are you planning to tell him about his daughter?"

"I said shut up," she shouted whirling to face the man behind her. "I won't do that to him as long as you people have her."

"Why not? With a little leverage, he could be useful to us." The man stepped onto the stage from the deep shadow in the back of the club. He reached out and touched Grace's shoulder in a possessive way.

She pulled away and laughed harshly. "If you think that, you don't know Sven Gulbrandsen."

The man touched her again, reinforcing his right to do so. She shuddered but didn't pull back again. "We know him very well. And you're right. If he knows about your little girl, he'll come after her. That may be to our benefit, under the right circumstances."

"He'll kill you."

"He'll try," the man corrected her. "And when he does, he'll draw Zack Mbele into it. And Mbele is the real target. We've gone to a lot of trouble to place you here just when Mbele's ship would be on Highpoint. If we decide Gulbrandsen should know about his daughter, you will tell him."

She stood rigid, head high, but said nothing.

The man chuckled softly. "Stiff necked as always." He stroked her hair once before turning and disappearing into the shadows again.

She heard the back hatch open and close as he left the club. Only then did her shoulders sag. She walked slowly to the piano and began playing. It was an old sad song about love and loss called "Red Sands."

AUTHOR'S NOTE

The preceding stories obviously dovetail, showing both Zack and Deuce's actions at the same time while the *Profit* is at Highpoint. Both of those stories become central later in this series. The next story is also available as a free downloadable e-book. It takes us back to events just after Zack's escape from Bruneault Prison at the end of the Reunification War. It was written for a short story exercise—one of those artificial set-ups where everyone in the group is given the same opening line and is given an hour to write a story from there. I was neck deep in *Thieves Profit* at the time, and this is what popped out.

INITIAL PROFIT

Lu Chin opened the hatch and prepared to step in, when she noticed a shadow inside her ship. She raised her gun toward the shadow when someone, or some thing, knocked it out of her hand. The needler clattered onto the metal deck and disappeared into the darkness of the unlit forward shuttle bay.

She spun toward the shadow and crouched in a fighting stance.

She caught a glimpse of shining white teeth in a mahogany dark face that looked at her with an air of pity. Then a massive fist crashed into the side of her head and her vision went blacker than the darkness of the Martian night outside.

"I dunno, LT," said a deep baritone voice that seemed to echo in Lu Chin's head. "Maybe, I hit her too hard."

She lay on her back on a surface that was softer than the deck but still dug uncomfortably into her back and shoulders. She held still, trying to gather as much information as she could while they thought she was still unconscious. Her head hurt. The left side of it pounded with each heartbeat, sending waves of pain around her skull, down her neck, and into her jaw. She wanted desperately to move her arms but forced herself to remain still as she tried to control her breathing.

"Don't worry, Deuce," said a second voice, this one more cultured and slightly higher pitched into the tenor range. "She's awake. She's playing dead, aren't you Ensign?"

Lu Chin sighed and opened her eyes. Two men stood over her. One was huge and blond. His head was shaved but his beard was long enough to touch his chest and was drawn into two tight braids. He looked down at her anxiously, his eyes filled with a concern that looked out of place on his square, scarred face.

The second man was as dark as the giant was light. He was slim and athletic, but his face had a gauntness that spoke of recent pain and hunger. His eyes were dark, almost black, and looked sunken beneath the high cheekbones. His skin was the color of polished mahogany and his black hair fell in long dreadlocks to his lithe, muscular neck.

He looked into her eyes and smiled, showing full lips and even white teeth. "Welcome back, Ensign. Sorry to surprise you like that, but we're very popular with the Federation Provosts right now and didn't want you sounding an alarm. Are you all right? Deuce was afraid he'd killed you." He indicated the blond giant with a slight tilt of his head.

"Didn't know she was a girl," muttered Deuce.

"She's not a girl, Deuce. She's an Ensign in what's left of the Martian Navy and I'm guessing this is her ship. Where is the rest of the crew, Ensign?"

Lu Chin didn't answer right away. She shifted on what she now recognized as a bunk in the enlisted berthing area. She twisted around and tried to sit up, only to realize her hands were bound behind her back with flexicuffs. She shot an angry look at the dark man.

He smiled again and twitched his right hand up to show her the needler in it. Her needler.

He nodded. "Yes, that's the way it is. Now, why don't we start again? Who are you and where is the rest of your crew?"

Lu Chin looked at the needler for a half second more. The man pointed it at her head.

"Bao Lu Chin," she said quickly. "And there is no other crew. The other officers were reassigned and the enlisted crew deserted when the Feddie landings started." That was close to the truth. Except that Ensign Hamilton was dead and it was her uniform that Lu Chin was wearing.

"So why did you stay, Ensign Bao? By the way, your collar devices are upside down."

"Someone had to be in charge," she said. "This ship is Republic property and you're trespassing."

The dark man laughed, a rich musical sound that made her spine tingle. "Did you hear that, Rabbit. We're bona fide enemies of the state now. We're trespassing on Navy property."

From above, in one of the upper bunks, she heard a wheezing, whining sound that might have been the laugh of a small nervous dog. She looked up and saw a thin, pale face staring down at her from over the edge of the top bunk. "We're wanted men. We have the death penalty on three systems." He let out another insane little laugh.

Lu Chin didn't see what was funny, but both the dark man and the one called Deuce smiled. A cold knot of fear tightened in her gut. These men were crazy and she was their prisoner.

The dark man seemed to sense her distress. "Relax, Ensign. No one is going to hurt you, as long as you don't get in our way. What happened to your ship? Most of the fast interceptors should have been captured or destroyed in the Federation assault."

"We took a hit during a scouting mission a month ago." Lu Chin decided the truth was easier than any story she could concoct. "It took out the aft shuttle bay and fried the pulse generators and fire control systems. We barely made it back to Mars. The dockyard in Planetia replaced three whole frames in the after hull and half of the starboard stringers were warped. They had to pull all the pulse generators and missile tubes to get at them. The ship's pretty much an empty hull with engines right now. It was transferred here to have the weapons systems reinstalled. Except, there were no systems to put in. So the crew was reassigned and I was left with a few ratings to babysit it."

The dark man cocked his head and regarded her for a moment. "Deuce, cut her loose."

Deuce reached behind her and she felt the flexcuffs release. She brought her hands slowly from behind her back and rubbed her wrists.

"My name is Zachariah Mbele," said the dark man. "Once upon a time, I was a First Lieutenant in the Special Operations Corps, Counter Insurgency Unit. Lately, I've been just another *lech* in Bruneault Prison. This is First Sergeant Deuce Gulbrandson," He pointed to the blond giant, who nodded his head toward Lu Chin but didn't speak. Mbele indicated the small man in the upper bunk. "And that is Rabbit, otherwise known as Eddie Conejo, also a former *lech.*"

"Lech?"

Mbele smiled. "It's an old Russian word, late 20th century. It means 'prisoner,' with political overtones."

"What do you want with me?"

Mbele twitched the needler in her direction. "The release codes for the ship's AI pilot. You see, we intend to steal her, along with the ten kilos of platinum in her aft hold."

Lu Chin cursed under her breath. They'd found the platinum. She'd intended all along to take the ship, the metal, and make a run for the Belt. It had been such a simple plan, until Hamilton had decided to be a hero and got herself shot before she could tell Lu Chin the release code. "I don't have them. I'm just a babysitter. We weren't supposed to be flying anywhere, so the AI is locked down."

Mbele gave her a strange look, then shifted his gaze to her collar devices and smiled. "Okay. We do it the hard way."

Lu Chin felt a surge of fear but steeled herself not to flinch. Instead of striking her, Mbele reached out toward the upper bunk. Rabbit slithered off the bunk and onto Mbele's back like a child getting a piggy-back ride.

"Can't move my legs," Rabbit said to her. Then he giggled again.

"Can you crack the security code for this ship?" Mbele shifted to balance Rabbit's weight on this back.

Rabbit snorted derisively. "I wrote most of it. I told you we didn't need any stinking codes. I can slice that pilot open in under a minute and have us airborne in three. You know, Zack, we really don't need her. Once I get through the..."

"Enough, Rabbit," said Mbele with surprising gentleness. "Deuce, take Rabbit up to the cockpit, then find a dorsal access hatch and give us some overwatch cover with your pulse rifle."

"Right, LT. What about the girl?"

"Let me worry about that. We may not have much time before either the Fed Provosts or some other crooks with the same idea we have show up. I don't want a firefight if we can avoid it."

Deuce shifted Rabbit from Mbele's back to his own and left the compartment.

Lu Chin watched them go, then looked back at Mbele. He was pointing the needler at her again. She froze as she saw the weapon and the cold glint in his eye.

"I don't want to shoot you. But Rabbit is very good and he'll probably unlock the ship's AI in a minute or two, so why don't we try the truth this time."

"What do you mean?" Lu Chin tried one last time to bluff it out but could see he wasn't buying it.

"Any ship's officer would have the release codes. You'd need them to do any work on the fire control systems or security grid. And no Ensign more than a day out of OCS would put those collar devices on upside down." He paused and looked around the compartment. "What are you? Hull tech? That bunk over there has been used recently. Yours?" He pointed directly at Lu Chin's bunk. She hadn't been able to open Hamilton's cabin so she'd stayed in her own bunk the last two nights.

"Fire control technician." She avoided his hard eyes. "Ensign Hamilton was the OIC, and I was supposed to help with the weapons interfaces. But the new weapons systems never arrived and all the other techs ran when the Fed fleet got control of the high orbitals. Hamilton ordered me to come with her when the landings started. She got shot trying to take out one of the landing craft with a Lancer missile pack."

"But you survived. Is that her uniform?"

Lu Chin lifted her head defiantly. "I'm no coward. There wasn't anything I could do for the Ensign, and the Marines had pinpointed our location. I got out just as the cluster grenades hit. I found her spare uniform in the laundry and figured an officer would pull more weight than a Second Class tech."

Mbele laughed out loud. "You were going to take the platinum and the ship for yourself."

"So what if I was? I found the platinum in the warehouse. I'm the one who moved it into the hold. The only reason I'm still here is that Hamilton got herself shot before I could get the release codes from her."

Mbele laughed again and lowered the needler. "I like your style, Second Class Petty Officer Bao. I'll make you an offer. You go on playing an Ensign. We may need a face to show officialdom when we fly out of here. Once we sell the platinum, I'll pay you a ten percent finders fee and drop you off in Planetia. I have a contact there who's buying the platinum. You can be on your way from there."

Lu Chin held his gaze, not flinching this time. "Fifteen percent and you take me with you when you leave Mars."

"Who says we're leaving?"

It was Lu Chin's turn to laugh. "If the Provosts are looking for you, then you're in trouble with both the Feds and Metternich's people. I can't see you lot hanging around Mars when you have a ship that can outrun almost anything in space. Mars is finished. I want out."

Mbele held out his hand. "Deal."

Lu Chin took his hand, but before she could say anything more, the ship's intercom squawked.

"I've sliced the pilot program and cleared the security blocks, Zack," Rabbit said over the intercom. "We can lift anytime you say, but you'd better come up here. We've got company."

Mbele punched the reply key. "I'm on my way. Is Deuce topside?"

"He's on the upper hull in a pressure suit, just in case somebody gets cute or careless and depressurizes the hanger."

"Right. Seal all the hatches. We're coming up."

"We? You mean the girl and you? Is that a good idea? I mean, she's pretty and all, but..."

Mbele shut the intercom off, ending what promised to be a long objection from Rabbit. Lu Chin followed him out into the forward shuttle bay and up the ladder to the second deck. Rabbit was in the cockpit, still talking into the intercom when they arrived. He looked up at her and giggled.

Lu Chin did her best to ignore him and looked out through the forward viewscreen. Three men in pressure suits stood in front of the bow of the ship. The hanger door seals activated with a hiss of cold mist, and the big indicator on the far wall shifted from red to green.

"Those are Federal suits," said Lu Chin. "Provosts? Or regular military."

"If those are Fed Provosts, then I'm the President of Mars," Mbele replied. "They're toting Martian made pulse rifles and have no unit insignias."

The man in the middle slung his pulse rifle on his shoulder and loosened his helmet seals. Mbele sighed as the man lifted the helmet and slung it from the strap on the suit's belt.

"Clancy," he said, as if he had expected it.

"Who's Clancy?" Lu Chin was suddenly worried about her cut. If this Clancy had any official juice, her position was in jeopardy.

"He was a guard in the Bear, that is, Bruneault Prison," Mbele said softly. "And one of three men I swore to kill before I die. Open the starboard hatch, Rabbit. I'm going out."

"I'm coming, too," said Lu Chin, not willing to let Mbele talk to Clancy without being able to hear what was said.

Mbele looked at her and opened his mouth as if to reply. Then he shut it and nodded. He handed her the needler. "Deuce will be covering us from above. Don't shoot unless he does, understood?"

Lu Chin nodded and followed him out of the cockpit. They left the ship and walked side by side toward the three suited figures. Lu Chin was acutely aware of her lack of a pressure suit and hoped nobody was carrying a projectile weapon. Mbele seemed unconcerned. He walked casually, even smiling at Clancy as they approached.

Clancy pulled a short-barreled pistol from his belt and pointed it at them. "That's close enough, Mbele. Who's the girl?"

"I'm Ensign Bao Lu Chin, Martian Navy, and you're trespassing on Navy property."

"Shut up, girlie." Clancy shifted the pistol her way. "I wasn't talking to you."

"Mind your manners, Clancy," said Mbele softly. "This isn't the Bear. You're on my ground now."

Clancy laughed. "Hear that, boys? His ground." He stepped forward, pressing the pistol up under Mbele's chin. The other two men leveled their pulse rifles at Lu Chin. "This is my ground now, and I ain't scared of no *lech*. When I finish gutting you, I'll do for your girlfriend next."

Lu Chin wasn't sure what happened next. One second Mbele was rising up on his toes as the pistol pushed up under his jaws. The next he was moving faster that her eyes could track him. He grabbed the pistol, forcing Clancy's hand to the right. Clancy fired but the muzzle now pointed at his partner, not Mbele. The man to Clancy's right was knocked backward by the bullet, which shattered his chest plate and punched through his heart. He dropped to the deck.

Lu Chin dove to her left, hearing the crackle of a pulse rifle. As she hit the hanger deck and rolled, she realized the shot had come from behind her. She came to her feet, aiming her needler at Clancy's second partner.

She didn't shoot. The man had let his own weapon fall as he gazed, open mouthed, at the smoking hole in the middle of his chest. His hands flapped feebly before he fell and lay still.

Lu Chin swept her aim left toward Clancy, but Mbele had him by the throat. The pistol was on the deck, and Clancy clutched at Mbele's right hand as it gripped his neck. Mbele squeezed tighter and lifted Clancy off his feet, holding him with impossible strength at an arm's length. Clancy's eyes bulged and his face darkened to a purple hue.

"LT?" Deuce called from above and behind Lu Chin. She looked back to see him standing on the ship's upper hull, just above the cockpit. "Don't do it, LT. He ain't worth it."

Mbele cocked his head and looked into Clancy's bulging eyes. "What do you say, Clancy? Should I listen to him?" He sighed and lowered the other man to the deck. He didn't loosen his grip. "You weren't there, Deuce. You don't know what this guy did."

"So turn him over to the Provosts. That's their job," said Deuce.

"Can't do that, Deuce. I promised myself. I promised Rabbit and all the rest of the *lechs* on that cellblock." He shifted his grip to Clancy's chin and placed his left hand on the back of Clancy's head. Clancy took a deep, rasping breath. Then Mbele moved his hands sharply.

Lu Chin heard the snap three meters away. Clancy jerked and then slid limply to the deck.

* * *

Sixteen days later, a credit chit for ten thousand *yuan* in her kit bag, she watched as Mbele negotiated with a forger on a backwater asteroid called Delilah.

For a while, during their trip out, she'd tried to make a play for him. He was attractive enough, and she had nowhere else to go. But he had closed himself off after killing Clancy.

Deuce and Rabbit were nice enough, but she felt out of place in their tight group of shared pain and experience. She had passage on a shuttle to O'Neil and a possible job lined up with a weapons manufacturer there. It had been a profitable three weeks, but she needed something more settled than a berth on an itinerant freighter.

The forger had agreed to Mbele's price and was putting the finishing touches on new ownership papers for the stolen ship.

"And what name should I put down for the ship registration?" he asked.

"Profit," Mbele replied. "Call her the Profit."

ACKNOWLEDGMENTS:

Many thanks to Bob Nelson of Brick Cave Media whose continued friendship and support made this collection possible.

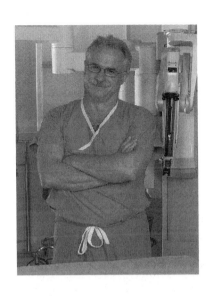

ABOUT THE AUTHOR:

Bruce Davis is a writer of Science Fiction and Fantasy. His current books, published by Brick Cave Media, include the Magic Law series of which Silver Magic is the third installment. It, along with Platinum Magic and Gold Magic are a mash-up of High Fantasy and Police Procedural set in a modern world. Also published by Brick Cave are his Profit Logbook series of SF novels about Zach Mbele, former Martian special forces commando and captain of the fast freighter, the Profit.

In his day job, he is a Trauma and Critical Care surgeon at a Phoenix area Level 1 Trauma Center. His independently published non-fiction memoir Dancing in the Operating Room is a glimpse into the life and training of a Trauma Surgeon.

He lives in Mesa, AZ with his wife who tolerates his passions for writing, science fiction conventions, kayaking, and collecting functional swords and custom knives.

Made in the USA
Columbia, SC
05 December 2024

47452124R00061